IMPERMANENT FACTS

Edited by
Amanda Saint

Copyright © 2018 The authors and Retreat West Books
Print Edition

First published by Retreat West Books in 2018

Apart from use permitted by UK copyright law, this publication may only be reproduced, stored, or transmitted, in any for, or by any means, with prior permission by email of the publishers; or in the case of reprographic production in accordance with the terms of license issued by the Copyright Licensing Agency.

All characters in the publication are fictitious and any resemblance to real persons, living or dead, is purely coincidental.

ISBN eBook: 978-1-9997472-9-9
ISBN print: 978-1-9997472-0-6

Retreat West Books
https://retreatwestbooks.com

For readers and writers of short stories

FOREWORD

I'm delighted to be publishing the second anthology of winners from the annual Retreat West Short Story and Flash Fiction Prizes and to see a couple of authors from the first one appearing here again.

Well done to all of the writers whose stories appear here as they made the Top 10 out of hundreds of entries. But particularly to those who received the top three prizes and a highly commended.

Alison Moore was the judge for the short story competition and she chose Karen Featherstone's *Calvo Marsh* as the overall winner, saying of it: 'I admired this clever, jocular and painful story about a nighttime journey into coastal marshland and the narrator's disintegrating sense of identity.

She awarded second prize to *Home Improvements* by Joanna Campbell. 'A child's-eye view of a troubled marriage, with a well-constructed and deftly controlled narrative and a poignant ending.'

Third Prize went to the *The Distance* by Keren Heenan and Alison said: 'A sensitive and touching exploration of the complex and shifting relationship between a daughter and her ageing mother.'

Alison also chose highly commended *An Entry in the Yellow Book* by Dianne Bown-Wilson, saying 'The intrigue builds to an unexpected ending that is both satisfying and haunting.'

Tania Hershman took on the task of choosing the winning flash stories and it was Jude Brewer's *When My Wife Is Out Of Town* that got the top spot. Tania said: 'This story grabbed me right away from the title, it promises so much, it's bursting with tension, and it tells you so much! It takes risks in its structure, going off on tangents, not following a linear narrative, and the risks pay off. It is dark and funny and moving and strange.'

Second place went to *Impermanent Facts* by Lucie McKnight Hardy for a story that is: '…such a beautiful piece, which takes place over a few minutes and a whole lifetime. The most important thing is that this story is almost unbearably moving precisely because it doesn't look straight at the Terrible Thing at its heart, until that one line at the end. The bulk of this gorgeous short short story is about ladybirds. But of course it isn't. Stunning.'

And the third-place spot is *The City of Stories* by Tamar Hodes. Tania said: 'Great title, and from the opening line the writer sets the scene and sets the tone. We think we know what kind of story this is, a traditional village tale. But then a few lines in, all our expectations our overturned, narratively-speaking, and we find that this is metafiction, it's a story about stories and about the danger of cliches, and it makes its point wonderfully, amusingly and in just as many words as needed and no more.'

I chose *Impermanent Facts* as the title as it just seemed so fitting for the times we are living in when the media is filled with fake news and what appears to be 'a fact' one day is shown to be anything but the next. Also because fiction is a form of facts as we dip into these characters lives – the stories and the people may be made up but the insights they give us into the human condition are always true.

Amanda Saint

CONTENTS

Foreword by Amanda Saint	v
The City of Stories by Tamar Hodes	1
Calvo Marsh by Karen Featherstone	3
Inside Story by Sandra Arnold	15
An Entry in the Yellow Book by Dianne Bown-Wilson	17
Not My Fault by Melvyn Elridge	31
Curl Up And Die by Alison Wassell	33
Options for the Ridiculously Poor by Ian Tucker	35
Thou Shalt Not Kill by Bettina Daniel	47
Chronic by Sarah Baxter	65
Boys Outside by Laurence Jones	67
Cinders After Midnight by Shirley Golden	81
Home Improvements by Joanna Campbell	83
Impermanent Facts by Lucie McKnight Hardy	91
Roast Potatoes by Rachael Dunlop	93
The Distance by Keren Heenan	103
The Land of Bondage by Bettina Daniel	115
The Martha Rhymes by Susan Breall	125
Time, Difference, Japan by Jason Jackson	137
We Don't Understand The Machines We Have Created by Olivia Fitzsimons	141
While My Wife Is Out Of Town by Jude Brewer	145
Author Biographies	147
Acknowledgements by Amanda Saint	153

The City of Stories
Tamar Hodes

Rosa, the village gossip, visited her friend Gretel's market-stall where herring and sardines shimmered silver in the bright sun.

'Have you heard?' whispered Rosa, leaning forward. 'Hilda's had her baby. There's been some devilry and the baby's an elephant.'

Gretel frowned and stepped back. 'You know, Rosa. I'm rather tired of my reputation as the gossipy fish-wife who trades in tittle-tattle. I'm not just a fictional construct. Ask someone else.'

Disappointed, Rosa walked to the city fountain where water spurted in huge white arcs. There she saw Trega lying on the stone steps. His feet were bare and his clothes dirty.

'Have you heard?' said Rosa, bending towards him and wincing at the smell. 'Hilda's had her baby. There's been some devilry and the baby's an elephant.'

Trega winced. 'You know, Rosa. I'm rather weary of my reputation as the poor village idiot who surprisingly spouts wisdom. I'm not just a narrative device. Ask someone else.'

Worn-out and frustrated, Rosa sought out the blind prophet, Manga. He sat, as he always did, with his white cane and yellow dog by the green statue.

'Have you heard?' said Rosa, into his ear. 'Hilda's had her

baby. There's been some devilry and the baby's an elephant.'

Trega grimaced. 'You know, Rosa. I'm rather fed up with my reputation as the blind prophet who, despite his disability, can predict the future. I'm not just a mythological stereotype. Ask someone else.'

Dejected, Rosa walked on, past the temple with its striped globe-heads; past the theatre with its fantasy plays; past the library with its many stories; past the shack where the book group met each week. She did not imagine they wanted to hear the truth: they were too bound up in fantasy.

I know, she thought. I will ask Hilda myself: the horse's mouth and all that.

After a long walk across the busy city, she arrived at her friend's cottage. There she saw Hilda nursing her beautiful baby boy. He had a normal head, face and ears and no trunk.

'What a relief,' said Rosa. 'I'd heard there was devilry and the baby's an elephant.'

Hilda laughed. 'No: there's been a delivery and the baby's excellent. Trust you to distort the truth!'

Rosa squirmed. 'You know. I'm rather tired of my reputation as the village gossip who spreads bad news. I'm not just a folktale figurehead. I'm ready to relinquish that role.'

'Good,' said Hilda, passing her friend a glass of wine. 'I'll drink to that.'

So the baby sipped its milk and the women sipped their wine and they were at peace. Hilda told Rosa about the night-feeds and the dirty nappies, the bleak reality of it all.

These people did not live happily ever after because life is too complex and messy for that but they were all quite at ease in their city where no-one played their traditional roles any longer but were authentically, unashamedly, what they were.

A sort of happy ending.

Calvo Marsh
Karen Featherstone

BEFORE WE LEAVE, we laugh at ourselves because we like to think we're the sort of couple that would never go out at night, wearing head-torches, in a 14-year-old Skoda estate, to see natterjack toads. Correction: to listen to the mating calls of male natterjack toads.

The male natterjack (as well as being extremely rare) is famous for the loud, brazen racket he makes when attracting females in season. His call can carry on the wind over four kilometres, we have Googled. For Lily, we pretend to be more excited than we are and act comedy-naff, like the characters in Nuts in May. Gavin has fished out a bobble hat from somewhere.

We are too hip to be doing stuff like this. If it weren't for the fact that we're parents… Our child has derailed us. We used to be cool and now we are just humouring this dull, middle phase of our formerly exciting lives until Lily is grown and goes her own way. Then we'll pick up where we left off and be the people we were in our late twenties. Gavin and Amanda. Him in advertising and her a PR. Great couple. Before the recession, this was.

It's 11pm and I'm just finishing putting the waterproofs in the boot of the car, when Gavin steps out of the house with a red 1970's thermos.

'That probably contains asbestos,' I say. 'I don't want Lily drinking out of it.'

'But she's a beauty.' He pats the flask, as if he is the sort of man who refers to a Thermos as female.

'Ah yes, a chap is never alone with a thermos.' I answer, boorish, falling back into role. We smirk.

Gavin chucks the Thermos on the back seat next to Lily, who is belted up, swaddled in a down coat and wearing Ariana Grande-branded mittens. He settles into the driver's seat. 'You know, Mand,' he says, when I get in next to him, 'I expect we'll be telling our grandchildren one day about this trip.'

'I may throw myself into forming a natterjack appreciation society for the good people of the village. Natterjack-watch.' I laugh because, of course, we know I won't.

I don't know if Lily gets it when we speak like this, which is all of the time. Sometimes she will catch what we say and look confused or worried. I have tried to explain that Mummy and Daddy like banter; we don't mean any of it and we're just amusing ourselves. She is eleven. I have explained irony to her. She says her friends' parents don't talk to each other like this. We have left it there.

Our Skoda pulls out of our isolated farmyard and heads in the direction of the black, hump-backed fells, which, after all the years I have lived here, still look at night, to a city-born off-comer like me, threatening. I make myself remember what they look like in the day, their slopes gentle and soft like sleeping cats, in order to not feel apprehensive.

TO BE HONEST, we're hoping this outing will tick a lot of boxes. Firstly, you have to know that Lily goes to a grammar school and, believe what you like about grammar schools, our local one is full of rich people's children. There are more 4x4s in that school car park than at the local independent. The dads wear fruity-coloured corduroys at parents' evenings and display National Trust stickers in the back windows of (always less than 2 years-old) people-carriers.

Frankly, we can't keep up. While Lily's friends Jasmin and Leyla have gone respectively to the Dominican Republic and Las Vegas for their summer holidays, we have stayed in Cumbria, sowing vegetables on our allotment and sorting out the garage. A trip to the natterjacks is something we bet none of Lily's friends' parents will have thought of. They won't have been willing to get cold and dirty in ponds, to put the effort in.

That's how I persuaded Gavin to do this. If he could just spend a few hours away from his damned computer in the loft, a space he has commandeered for his extensive job-searching. I didn't want to moan. I know how hard he's been looking. He's even put a lock on the loft hatch to keep Lily away from his pens and stationary etc. because he likes to keep it all in order and systemised, but if he could spare a few hours away, I suggested, Lily would return home in the early hours of the morning with material for her Biology project on the life cycles of amphibians, and with data for her Geography assignment on coastal marshlands. And she'll have anecdotes about having been allowed to stay up all night, to rival her friends' holiday memories, which will no doubt be of their nannies tucking them up early in their beds while Mummy and Daddy got shit-faced in bars. This is what we hope happened on their holidays.

That's how I put it to him and he agreed, so we're going. For once, we feel ahead of the game. Does Lily see the strain of parenting that we try so well to hide? We are magicians not wanting the wires to show, so keen and hopeful are we to give her the ideal childhood one would want for an only child. There will be no second chance to get it right.

ALSO, I SHOULD mention, there is one last box for this trip to tick. Something appalling happened recently, at Lily's school, and Gavin and I feel we should redeem ourselves. Lily came home on the last day of term before the summer break, and said she had told her deputy head-teacher, who happens to be from Nigeria, that we, Gavin and I, can't tell the difference between one black person and another because, to us, they all look the same.

Now. Let me explain. I have already said how Gavin and I, we have a unique way of communicating with each other. We don't take things too seriously. To explain further, I have already illustrated what the parents at Lily's school are like. Gavin and I pretend we are like that. It's harmless and it keeps us entertained. We sometimes pretend we are huntin' and shootin' types and that we have a gun-dog called Nigger. We don't own a dog and we have never been shooting.

When we gave our imaginary dog that name, we were trying to think of the worst, most awful name a person could ever give a dog. We chose the most insensitive, politically unaware, offensive, vile term. Because (and I have never explained this out loud to another soul, so bear with me) it's just something we fall into. We speak as if we're the kind of people who would say abominable things. I suppose it gives us a perverse reassurance that we are safely nothing like those people.

So this one time a couple of months ago, I was telling Gavin that he should take Nigger for a walk to the village shop because the rice situation was getting out of hand (another expression which amuses us; we had simply run out) when Lily looked up and said she thought we had used a bad word. She asked exactly what nigger meant and we told her it was an old-fashioned term used to describe a black person and that it was now considered very offensive. She asked why we had said it then, and we explained that it makes us laugh to act as if we're the sort of people who would ever say such a thing, because of course we absolutely aren't. She was looking bewildered, so we gave examples of black people who are role models and who have achieved great things, like Denzel Washington and the one who was in Luther, in order to demonstrate that we are really, not at all, by any stretch of the imagination, racist. Then Gavin said, "Mind you, they all look the same to me." And he laughed. At himself, of course. I'm afraid I laughed too. And we thought that was the end of the matter. Until Lily repeated what Gavin had said at school.

The deputy head teacher is new in her post. Lily will be at the school for another six years. I have thought about going in to see the teacher, Miss Daramola, to explain, but however I imagine our meeting going, it ends badly. Gavin would never go in. At any cost, he avoids confrontation.

So when we heard the school had planned a trip to see the natterjack toads at Calvo Marsh, but that it had had to be cancelled due to the mini-bus breaking down, Gavin and I thought that if we made the trip, it would seem like we are great parents, at least. It would show we're magnanimous and that we think of others' children as well as just Lily. We thought we could record the sounds of the toads, you see, make some slides and offer a brief presentation during a break-time for pupils who have been unfortunate enough never to have experienced the elusive natterjacks. We thought that Miss Daramola might think she had misunderstood what Lily had said. Or that, being a child, Lily had simply misheard us. And considering Lily's problems, Miss Daramola might then give us the benefit of the doubt.

We are driving into blackness. As the car's headlights slice through it, Lily, in the back, snores softly. I think this is the first time in ages we have done anything together, really together. And it's certainly the first time I can remember being awake with

Gavin at this time of the night. Normally I go to bed before him and, somehow, he is there next to me come morning. Although I never remember him getting in. Ships in the night.

Of course, Lily is too young to understand all the nuances of the situation at school. Or she is too earnest. Or she is mildly autistic. There. I've said it. I think she is somewhere on the spectrum. Because sometimes she will have a look on her face, so sweet and other-worldly, as if she really does inhabit a different or higher plane. And she doesn't understand Gavin and I. She really doesn't get us at all. The things she comes out with. Her statements are bold, so stark. If she doesn't like someone she'll say it. It she loves something, she'll come right out and say that too. Sometimes she'll shout it. It's like she hasn't picked up how to have proper conversations. Gavin won't have her tested. I am just being patient, waiting to see if she develops more as predicted as she matures. But it's a worry.

So there is a lot riding on this trip. By the time we head past Silloth, the coastline's smooth sweeping lines can only be imagined by the snaking of the car as it's too dark outside to see a thing. It's nearing 11pm. Ariana Grande's Dangerous Woman album (Lily will listen to nothing else, over and over again; another bad, OCD-like sign, I feel) is annoying me with its lyrics of sexual prowess and what sounds to me like a bad case of over-confidence. I wonder what Lily makes of it all. The voice of this empowered, sexually liberated female, what could she possibly have to say to my pre-pubescent child?

Gavin takes a sharp turn onto what must be sand and the ground beneath the car's wheels feel softer, less certain. He drives confidently, but I feel alarmed, like I've been paddling in shallows and have stepped off a hidden shelf in a black ocean and my feet can't find the bottom.

'What if there's quicksand?' I ask.

'In West Cumbria? Don't be daft. We're not in Morecambe now, Toto.'

We've never been to Morecambe. This is one of those nights when nothing sits quite right. Nothing is obviously out of place, just things feel a bit off. Only in the subtlest of ways. Lily is plainly not quite excited enough to justify the length of the trip. She would rather have stayed in watching Dr Who on catch-up, I know, and so, if he were honest, would Gavin.

And you would think it funny if a family was visiting horny natterjacks and the parents were not having sex. The irony there would be unbearable. However, people are not technically speaking in a sexless marriage until they and their partner have sex fewer than 10 times per year, says Stylist magazine. More than ten times per year and you shouldn't complain.

Gavin picks up speed. We start to bump. It feels as though we are racing over sand dunes. The windows are black, but Gavin checks Googlemaps on his phone and announces that he thinks we've arrived. In 2016 it was 11 times. I wasn't counting. It may have been that I had read the Stylist article and so was unusually conscious of the frequency. That's roughly once every six weeks, so definitely not sexless.

Lily, it turns out, does not want to get out of the car. We agree she can sit in the back with the door open, to make use of the residual heat. A bit disappointing, but now I realise it has been more important to me that we make this trip than it has been to either of them and I wonder why this is. It takes a lot of motivation to open the car door and climb out of the heated interior into the cold, black night. A tang of salt in the air stings the back of my nostrils and the wind hushes through reeds. The cold seeps into the gap between my jumper and my waistband. My wrists are exposed. I see the veins in them, bluish in the moonlight, horribly vulnerable. Far off, the sounds of ewes baaing is familiar at least, or I might feel we have landed on a hostile moon. My God, look at the stars. How can I not have noticed them 'til now? Piercingly bright in the endless, depthless sky. I feel the immenseness of everything, when I look down again, I can't see my feet and am disorientated.

'Where are they then?' Gavin asks. 'I can't hear a thing. I thought they're supposed to be really loud? Are we in the right place?'

'I think so. Maybe we have to wait. Let's try and see the critters.' I aim the beam of my head torch across a shallow pond, only five or so centimetres deep. At first I see nothing, only short stubby grass and the glinting of the water, silty and opaque.

Then: 'I see them! I see something!' Gavin shouts.

Knobbly, thumb-sized heads, poking up through the pond's surface, their white gullets glowing in the murk of the water. Yet they are silent.

'I have heard the natterjacks singing. I do not think that they will sing to me,' says Gavin. He grins. He's so clever, I think, and all of a sudden I miss him powerfully, even though he's standing right here next to me. He decides to wait in the car and I say I will soldier on. It's bracing and I'll tell him and Lily as soon as I hear a sound. They sit in the car, cocooned in warmth and I turn my attention back to the silent toads.

I couldn't be in a sexless relationship. I think about sex a lot, if I'm honest. I suppose if we did it more, I might think about it less, but it's hard to say. You do obsess more about things that aren't there. If I lose my reading glasses, until I have them back again, they're all I think about. Behind me, I hear Gavin opening the door again. He calls out to me from the driver's seat.

'I'm a bit worried about draining the battery, so I won't put the lights on, even though I still can't see a fucking thing,' he says.

'Don't swear in front of Lily,' I answer automatically.

'Dad,' I hear Lily say, her voice slightly muffled from her coat which she has zipped right up to cover her mouth. She pulls it down, so her voice is much clearer now. 'Dad, do you watch porn?'

Something hangs finely balanced in the air. Through the reeds, the wind feels their stalks, their ears, considering them, as though the wind is deciding which way to blow.

I hear Gavin say: 'No. I have never done that.'

Lily continues: 'Because Jasmin said that over ninety-five percent of men do… and the other five percent are lying!' Oh Lily, the awful jarring. The shortfall between what I hoped you would be before I had you and who you have become. I listen to you sometimes and ponder the odd, inappropriate, sitting not-quite-right comments and I am pained.

Gavin's face begins to climb out of the protective bunker into which his features have sunk. It registers; she was telling a joke. It was an opener to a humorous remark and he needn't have answered. At the very least he needn't have added the "I have never done that." That last bit, honestly. No would have been enough. Never was overkill.

I CLOSE MY eyes and if it weren't for my goosepimples, the dank in my nostrils, the swampy feel underfoot, I could almost be back on honeymoon with Gavin in St Lucia. The repetitive sounds I hear are not of natterjacks but of…what? Yes, cicadas and tree frogs of the unbelievable, technicolour landscape. I hear waves gently lapping now, the waiter carrying rum to us in clinking glasses on a tin tray, my unread paperback warming, fingerprinted with the excess of suntan oil rubbed on my shoulders by Gavin. He hadn't been able to keep his hands off me. I caught him staring at me through a gap in the bathroom latch as I dressed, and he said he wouldn't apologise as I was too beautiful. Honeymoon words, syrupy, golden as the light that streaked across our skin in the mornings, an abundance of everything; light, food, sun, warmth, time, ourselves. Nothing was too much. Where has all this of us gone?

I consider my position. What will I say to him? In the car, perhaps while Lily sleeps in the back seat, or in bed tonight. With ten inches of sheet between us, and something finely balanced in the air, I should make a joke of it. I should share his mortification at what Lily has said. I imagine sharing the anecdote with other parents, on a boozy evening out, or at a wedding. Perhaps Gavin will use it in a speech giving Lily away at hers. And we'll laugh and cover our faces remembering and Lily will squirm. But something has risen in me. It is in my throat and I swallow, but it is still there. I don't know what it is, but it cannot be mock-mortified away. I don't know if I will say anything to him tonight. It may be that I let it lie, like the icebergs that loom under the surface of a marriage ready to wreck the blindly happy, or the ones who just need to know, the spouses fatally demanding to be heard and proven right. As if rightness will be enough when rightness is what I am left with.

I open my eyes. Back in Silloth promise falls away. This place is saying: I know what St Lucia offered you, but you have this. This is it. And all the decisions of your life, big and small, led to this, here, now. And I want to say, yes, but I didn't know at the time – no one told me that all the tiny compromises and misfirings and interruptions and shortcuts and giving-ups, that these were the pixels that make up the final photo. No one said. All the time that went so fast but felt it dragged. Always I've been waiting for a next thing – a better thing or time. I should be where I want to be, here, now. I should be happy with my lot. Or

I should shut up.

I want him. I want Gavin. I want him to pull me into the night and kiss me and know me and I want to know him and to have what we had and be who we were. I am sick of pretending and laughing at ourselves.

From the car, Gavin catches my eye. We grin at each other as though… Oh, I'm too tired to think of what sort of couple we are like. I climb into the passenger seat and our little stick family sits in silence all the way home.

Back in the yard, a far-away dog barks. Or is it nearby, on a neighbouring farm? The noise rebounds like a slap against the backs of the fells in this land-locked valley, so that I can't tell what direction the sound comes from. Once again, I feel disorientated. I don't like the night. Not since I moved here. I have no sense of what's true in a country night. Give me honest buildings and curbs any day, or a tropical sea that whispers escape.

Inside Story

Sandra Arnold

IN THE CITY there were too many voices. Loud. Discordant. She couldn't make sense of them. In the daylight their clamour ensured she walked into lamp posts, forgot appointments, drifted off at traffic lights. At night she lost sleep trying to fit all the pieces together.

So she left the city for the countryside. For an old house with a garden. To clear a space for herself. To listen. To think. In this place, where noise meant distant sheep and the occasional tractor rattling down the gravel road, she learned to listen differently. She learned to trust what she heard.

Sometimes she'd find herself kneeling in the flower beds, gripping her trowel until her fingers turned blue, unwilling to move until she knew exactly where the dead pets were buried and the ashes of a longed-for baby; until she understood the broken dreams of the couple whose initials were carved on the plane tree; saw the love letters burning in the bin; heard the children singing in the river before the sudden silence; watched the old woman at the mailbox reading her son's last letter; saw the old man so intent on videoing his young wife with the hitchhiker that he didn't see who put rat poison in his tea.

Friends came to visit. They expressed doubts. Perhaps a little too quiet? Not much happening? A bit dull? She marvelled that they couldn't hear what was rising up through tree roots, creeping beneath bark, whispering inside leaves.

An Entry in the Yellow Book
Dianne Bown-Wilson

IN THE BLACK text imprinted on the A5 page Hannah found something she hadn't been looking for. Like a genie unleashed from a bottle, she couldn't then un-find it, put it back, pretend she'd never seen it. Once read, it became a secret she was forced to carry with her and in the weeks that followed it taunted her like a toothache: *what are you going to do about me? What will you decide?*

Unsuspecting, she'd been flicking through the pages of *The Yellow Book*, the National Garden Scheme's directory of gardens open for charity. She bought it every year, partly as a charitable donation in itself and also because, now and again, the gardens were comfortable destinations for entertaining her husband's business visitors or their own friends. A drive to a different village, a leisurely stroll admiring whichever flowers or shrubs were in season, tea and cake; it was a diversion most people found difficult to dislike.

How could she have known?

The entry leapt out at her as she glanced at the photographs – beautiful in themselves, regardless of the locations of the gardens. *Thurbridge House*. Her throat tightened and she checked the address and description: *Over an acre of formal beds, pond, Victorian greenhouse, shrubs and orchard carefully renovated by the* new owners over the past two years. It *was* the place. Only the owners' names – Martin Clarkson and Tony Waller were unfamiliar. To the side of the address a yellow flag "NEW" indicated why she'd never seen it before.

Having moved out of Thurbridge almost thirty years earlier she'd never been back. Not to the house, the street, the town, or even within fifty miles of its location. She couldn't bear to. Now, here it was, beckoning to her: *Open Sunday 5 June (1-5). Adm £4, chd free. Home-made teas.*

IT WAS A Wednesday in March when Hannah made this discovery so she has weeks in which to make plans, or to decide to do nothing. Although the pressure of it aches like a physical pain, she mentions it to no-one. What could she say to Ludo, her husband? *I'm going back to have a look at the garden of the house where Jeremy and I lived. Yes, the one I pretend never existed. Why? Because now it's called out to me I can't not.*

But unable to put those thoughts into words, she stays silent. Neither does she say a word to any of her friends whom she knows would feel obliged to try and influence her decision. The only one she does think about telling is Marsha who knew her long before either Jeremy or Ludo came along.

I'm thinking of going to see Thurbridge, she'd say.

And no doubt Marsha, concerned and baffled, would reply, *Why? After all this time, is it wise?*

Probably not. But I've found a way I can just take a look and now I feel have to go.

Of course you don't.

But perhaps the reality will finally help me come to terms…

And perhaps not.

I'm still going.

Shall I come with you?

No.
Then take care, keep your distance, leave well alone.
She decides not to tell Marsha, either.

AS THE WEEKS pass Hannah finds herself faltering, fading, increasingly unable to eat or sleep. At the strangest hours of day and night, images of the Thurbridge garden pierce her thoughts with the insistence of a searchlight. Everything she planted there: roses, paeonies, delphiniums, lavender, box … she recalls each plant more clearly than anything else about the place. Around them all she'd dug hope and optimism into the soil like fertiliser, how long did it linger? Having failed to protect her did it work for them? She imagines the plants struggling and dying in their abandonment. She doubts their new owners understood their needs.

'Are you okay?' Ludo asks her one morning in May. 'You're not looking at all well these days and this not sleeping isn't you.'

If he's noticed, she must be looking bad, but she smiles reassuringly. 'I'm fine – time of life probably. Apparently, insomnia is the menopausal woman's burden.'

He grimaces and says no more. She'd known that any mention of women's trouble would silence him.

A week later, she lays the groundwork for a possible visit, intending – should she subsequently decide against it – simply to say that her plans haven't worked out.

'I'm thinking of going to see Marsha in a couple of weeks,' she announces to Ludo and Abby, their daughter, over dinner one night.

'Oh?' says Ludo.

'There's an exhibition near her that we both want to see, so I'm planning to go up on the Sunday morning, stay the night, and come back Monday.'

'Fine – hope you have a good time.' As such visits weren't uncommon, she'd accurately predicted his response.

'Let me know if you change your mind,' says Abby. At twenty-two she's their youngest child, and the last to leave home. As she frequently borrows her mother's car, this is the only inconvenience Hannah's being away will generate.

THE FOLLOWING SATURDAY, with both of them out, Hannah gives in to a compulsion that's been needling her for weeks. She pulls down the loft ladder, crawls up and retrieves a small suitcase that has lain there, unopened, since she and Ludo moved in twenty-five years earlier. She uses her sleeve to wipe off the worst of the dust and carries it to the loft hatch. As she struggles down with her burden she focuses intently on not falling, the last thing she needs is to have to explain.

On the landing where the light streams in, she fumbles in her pocket for the tiny key and unlocks the case. Immediately, she knows that all is as it should be. Packages of old photographs, a large envelope containing papers and certificates, a few cuddly toys in protective plastic bags, and a small collection of jewellery: wedding and engagement rings, a watch, a child's tiny bracelet. This is it then, she reflects. Eight years of my life. A husband, daughter, our dreams, hopes and plans. Only this remains.

She picks out an envelope of photographs and shakes them onto the carpet. She examines each one: Emma, a baby in her mother's arms – I look so young! Emma, a few months old, chuckling, being swung by Jeremy – he looks so carefree! Emma, her first birthday – she looks so happy…

For the next few hours Hannah sifts through it all. Every year of Emma's short life is captured, every major occasion – birthdays, Christmas, family visits – is here. She and Jeremy: in front of the house, in the garden, dressed up and going out – the two of them looking like…? Looking like strangers, she decides.

She inspects the papers: marriage certificate, divorce papers, Emma's birth certificate, Emma's death certificate. It's all here – a systematic archive of that part of her life that she's tried to eradicate, that different homeland that's now calling her back.

Eventually, flagging, she packs it all away, but driven by some force to keep these memories near she decides not to return the case to the loft. Instead, she slides it into a space at the back of her wardrobe where no-one else ever goes.

ON THE MORNING of Sunday, June 5th Hannah eases silently out of bed while Ludo still sleeps. 'I'll be setting off by eight,' she'd warned him the previous evening. 'I promised Marsha I'd be there first thing so we'd have the whole day.' Of course, with her actual destination only some 200 miles away, she doesn't need to leave so soon, but she's anxious to avoid the day – this very special day – being tainted by her current life.

The previous week, after much trying-on, she'd selected what she'd wear. An important decision as she suspects the new owners – this Martin and Tony – are probably quite exacting in their tastes and harsh in their judgements of others. Getting them to agree to what she wants will mean looking the part: casual yet stylish, a tad imposing. Linen would be the thing.

A fist of nervous apprehension clenches in her stomach as if she's heading off to a school reunion or maybe the wedding of a previous beau. But there's no possibility of running into anyone familiar here: all their old friends have gone, and they'd only ever known the neighbours as distant figures to whom, occasionally, they'd wave. It'll just be her and them.

With time to fill, Hannah drives carefully, steadily, stopping after about an hour in a small town she knows. There's a coffee shop there; it'll be quiet now, the staff preoccupied with preparing for the Sunday brunch rush.

She orders, chooses a table and takes out her phone. She scrolls up Marsha's number and taps in a message: *I've told Ludo and Abby I'm visiting you today. Should they make contact (v unlikely) please cover for me! Will explain later. Love xxx*

What will she explain? What will have happened by the end of today? She feels as if she's heading for an assignation with a lover, arranging to pass information to a spy, preparing to exterminate an adversary by slipping a dose of poison into his cup. Not that she has any idea what doing any of those things actually feels like but what she's about to do is equally out of character.

MUCH LATER, HAVING stopped several times to pass the hours, she turns into her old street and parks. She's still a few hundred yards from Thurbridge but she intends to proceed cautiously. After a couple of minutes, she takes a deep breath, gets out, and slowly strolls along the footpath toward the house.

Despite her years away, when she sees the place she's startled by how familiar it is. Reassuring or disturbing? – she can't decide. Someone has removed the hedge that once separated the front garden from the pavement and replaced it with iron railings but, otherwise, the exterior of the Georgian house is as it was. Only the windowsills and door – a faded blue when they'd moved in – are now a fashionable Farrow and Ball green.

She stands for a minute or two, gazing, taking it in, before crossing the road to follow an elderly couple who've just approached from the other direction. They stop at the gate where a

An Entry in the Yellow Book

young woman is collecting entrance fees. Hannah waits while she explains the garden layout to them and gives them directions to the tea room.

'One please,' she says, when the couple move away, 'And I heard all that, so you don't need to repeat it,' she smiles. 'Hopefully you've had a lot of visitors?'

'Mmm – loads. Good weather, so I guess that helps – although with Mart and Tony having done so much, everyone locally has come round to take a nosey at what they've been up to. Oops – you're not one of the neighbours are you?'

'No – I'm just passing through. And, obviously, you're not either Martin or Tony – are they about, or have they abandoned ship in the face of hordes of strangers?'

'Oh, they're here somewhere… you'll probably come across them round the garden; Mart's tall and thin with a ginger beard, and Tony – my uncle – is wearing the most awful purple flowery shirt. But don't tell him I said that.'

Hannah laughed, 'I won't.'

'Enjoy your visit, then.'

'I will.' Hannah is already walking up the drive, following the pull of her memories, heading past the side of the garage to where she hopes she'll still find the white rose arch next to the formal pond.

As she approaches, her heart racing, she can hardly bear to look – if it's gone, she suspects that the blow might fell her like a punch. But her fear is unfounded. The arch is still there and the rose itself, though old, seems flourishing. She studies the scene: the surrounding beds are a slightly different shape now, fuller than in their day; more beautiful, she has to admit.

For some minutes she stands there silently, fortunately no other visitors come near. Over thirty years ago she and Jeremy scattered their daughter's ashes under this arch in the expectation that they would live here, watching over her, for the rest of their lives. But within a year they were gone, abandoning all that remained. It was an act of betrayal for which Hannah has never been able to forgive herself.

'Are you Tony?' she forms her mouth into a warm smile. 'Your niece described you to me.'

'Sure am. Are you having a good look round?'

'Yes, I've been here a while so I think I've seen it all. That's why I came over – I'm leaving now and I wanted to say that I absolutely love what you've done. It's one of the most impressive gardens I've seen in a long time.'

'Oh, great,' he grins. 'Thanks for saying so. We've worked really hard and spent an absolute bomb on it, so it's good that it seems it's been worth the effort. Anyway, we adore it; I suppose that's what matters.'

'Yes, but I'd challenge anyone not to. You have such an eye for what works.'

'You're a gardener yourself then?'

'More an enthusiast than an expert, but seeing places like this always inspires me to learn more.'

'Hey, Tony!' A shout from the other end of the lawn cuts across their conversation. 'See you later – down the pub?'

'We'll be there.' Tony waves to the man, then turns back to Hannah.

Hannah breathes in deeply. This is it. 'You know,' she murmurs diffidently, gazing into the paeony border behind him, 'I used to live here in the eighties, it brings back quite some memories being here again.'

'Oh my God! *Really*? That's amazing. How long were you here?'

'Not as long as we intended. About eight years, and then circumstances changed and we had to move on. But it was a lovely house. It's been fantastic coming here and seeing it again. You've done so much.'

'Well, it was all in a real state when we got here, I don't think anyone had done anything to it for years. Oh, not that I mean that you hadn't, I'm sure you probably…'

'It was a terrible mess when we took it over, too. Then we did a lot – like you, reclaiming what had been here and re-planting – and refurbishing the interior. And then, as I say, we had to leave. I don't know how long the people we sold it to were here, or whether you bought it from them. I haven't kept in touch with anyone locally and this is the first time I've been back.'

The man, Tony, glances at his watch – a huge, clunky thing that Hannah estimates is probably worth more than all the jewellery she's ever owned. 'Look, I'm really sorry, I'd love to talk to you some more but there's a couple of people here that I promised to catch up with before they leave and I said I'd be with them in just a minute.' His apology seems genuine.

'That's fine. No problem, I shouldn't have waylaid you.' She pauses, willing herself to succeed. 'Look, I know this is terribly pushy of me, but I wonder if you'd be really, really kind and just let me have a fleeting look round the house? You've done such a marvellous job with the garden that I'd just love to see what you've done inside. It's such a wonderful place, I loved it so much while we were here, and it still means a lot to me to know that someone is loving it as much as we did. But, I understand if you'd rather I didn't; it's really quite unforgivable of me to ask…'

Fortunately, she's read him correctly. He can't resist showing off. 'No problem. I'm sure I'd feel the same way, and anyway, you don't look the type to run off with the family silver – not that we've got any! Just let yourself in through the back door, and if you come across Mart or anyone being difficult, tell them to have a word with me.'

'Oh thanks – you're *so* kind. I'll only be a very few minutes, I promise.'

'Enjoy!' He turns on his heel and makes off across the lawn. Immediately, Hannah sets off towards the back of the house.

Predictably, the interior feels much less familiar than the outside. The layout, doors, staircase are still the same but, as she'd anticipated, every aspect of the décor has altered. Although she and Jeremy had replaced just about everything when they moved in, that was a long time ago in interior design terms. Besides, it's evident from what they've done that these new owners aren't short of funds.

Her curiosity about most of the rooms is superficial; she takes in only what she can see while passing open doors. It's interesting to note what's changed, nothing more. Her target is the room upstairs at the back of the house, the one that used to be Emma's nursery, then bedroom, and now seems to be some sort of office or study. A modern desk and office chair, and a rather uncomfortable-looking sofa crouch in the space that used to be occupied by a child's bed and half-size wardrobe. No trace remains of the pink and white rabbit wallpaper and the fluffy cream carpet; the night-light stars on the ceiling are all gone.

Only the boarded-up Victorian fireplace is still there. The cast iron surround was white in their day, she'd painted it herself, now it's a dark slate grey. It was while painting it that she'd found the little enclosure, a tiny internal space between the inside board and the fire surround that was completely hidden from view yet capacious enough to take a smallish piece of paper, tightly folded.

She's on the floor now, ready to look, yet afraid of what she will – or won't find. The atmosphere around her, although it isn't a particularly warm day and the house is cool, suddenly becomes suffocating; memories, images, scents, sounds, start to crowd in.

Emma crying as she says goodbye. She has to go out, but Mummy won't be long, she'll come and give her a kiss as soon as she gets back – but she has to promise she'll be asleep.

She's got a temperature still but I've given her Calpol. I'll take her to the doctor tomorrow if she isn't better. But keep an eye on her, you know how young kids can suddenly get worse.

Jeremy, tired from long hours at work, grunting from behind his newspaper. Yeah, fine. Don't fuss, she's not a baby – she'll be okay.

When she'd come back, four hours later, Jeremy was still in the chair, newspaper slipped to the floor, snoring. Upstairs, Emma was covered in a scarlet rash, struggling to breathe.

IN THE MONTHS before Emma died, Hannah used to play the Fairy Game with her. It involved writing messages in spidery handwriting on tiny pieces of paper and leaving them in the hole in the fireplace for Emma to find.

Their content was simple:

Dear Emma,

Be a good girl and on Saturday Mummy might take you to see the ponies.

Love from Your Favourite Fairy.

Having originally helped Emma to 'find' the first message, Hannah subsequently persuaded her that this was the place that she should post requests – to the Tooth Fairy, Father Christmas, the Easter Bunny – which at the start, she'd helped her write. And then, as Emma's writing and reading improved and she began to suspect that the Fairy and her mother were one and the same, they both left more whimsical messages to read together. It was one of those that she'd found after Emma died.

Now, in this room, she can feel and see everything as clearly as if it happened only yesterday: rushing her to hospital – Jeremy driving like a lunatic while she cuddled Emma on her lap willing her to live; the long wait through the night with Emma in a coma and nothing to do but to watch the rise and fall of her chest as she struggled to breathe; the anguished faces of the hospital staff; the silent drive back the next day, knowing that this now was how it would always be.

She never said it, never needed to. She knew that he too felt it'd been his fault although, unprompted, the doctors had said that there was no certainty that Emma would have survived even if they had got her there earlier. But of course, it was her fault too, she'd gone out, left her; she never should have done that. She was her mother, she should have known.

When they'd come back from the hospital, both as stunned as each other, she'd gone straight to Emma's room. There, her bedclothes still lay in a heap and the scent of her still hung in the air. She remained there, virtually immobile, for the next two days, trying to hold on to what was left of her, unable to weep, attempting to understand.

After some hours a stray thought made its way through the thick blanket of grief in which she was swaddled. A message! From where she was sitting on the floor she crawled across to the fireplace. She could see there was something there and prised it from its hiding place. *Emma and Mummy 4 ever,* it said, in Emma's childish hand. Around it she'd drawn a heart shape and a border of flowers and kisses.

She'd sat holding it for what must have been hours before, eventually, she carefully refolded it and put it back where she'd found it, driven by an absolute need to leave everything in her daughter's room untouched.

When she and Jeremy sold the house less than a year later,

their relationship irretrievably shattered by their loss, she made the decision to leave it there still. She'd never told Jeremy about it; it was, had been, *their* secret – nothing to do with him.

HANNAH HEARS A door open downstairs and a man's voice shouts *Hello?* She knows she only has moments now to fulfil her mission. On the carpet, on her hands and knees in front of the fireplace, she can see the edge of the paper. Carefully she prises it out; it is fragile, yellowed, despite the urgency she unfolds it with care.

It is all as she remembers it: *Emma and Mummy 4 ever.*

But as she glances down, a fist grabs her heart and crushes the air from her lungs. Now, underneath it, in the same childish hand are new words, *I miss you Mummy.*

For a few seconds, the room swims, a band tightens round her throat.

She hears the man approaching: *Hello, are you there?* She gasps for air. Panicking, hands trembling, she refolds the paper and pushes it back. Something tells her she must leave it here, but unable to make sense of what she's seen, she's conflicted.

As she scrambles to her feet the door opens.

'Everything okay?' Tony, the man she met earlier, looks quizzical.

She speaks robotically, with the ease of a habitual dissembler. 'Yes, sorry. Just had to take a call and I dropped my phone.'

Tony shrugs.

'But the house is looking fabulous; thank you again for letting me look round.' Despite her pounding heart, her tone is smooth.

He smiles.

She knows that nothing's happened here that she can tell anyone about, nothing that can be explained, or that anyone would believe. She can hear their voices now: *You must have been mistaken, it's been a long time. Easy for one's mind to play tricks…*

'I really must go,' she says, backing out of the room. 'Congratulations again on making it into the Yellow Book.'

Not My Fault
Melvyn Elridge

IT BEGAN WITH a dinner to launch a battlefield helicopter. The top table seated Generals, together with local and national politicians. My boss Derek and his wife sat with them. Yes, I suggested my table guests fold menu cards into paper airplanes. We ran along in front of the top table to launch our squadron. A surprised waiter jumped and spilt fruit summer pudding over the Brigadier General and his wife. The top table went into meltdown. I did not see how it had been my fault.

Once the fracas calmed, I slipped outside for a quiet drink. But along comes Derek's wife. Not my fault one thing led to another. When Derek found us, her arms were around my neck, lips pressed to mine, her legs wrapped around my waist. She started it. If Jean had not told him to clear off I might have got away with it.

The next morning in front of Derek, I expected a slap on the wrist.

He said, 'Gordon, you're fired.'

It had been a bit of harmless fun. I cleared my head with a walk on the seafront where an idea formed. I threw paper pieces in the air. Whatever way the wind blew them, I would follow.

On the Eurostar to Paris the lady next to me, attractive brunette, mid-forties, asked my destination. She noticed me reading the Stamp Collectors Quarterly. We chatted amiably. I helped her off the train in Paris where she gave me a long stare.

'Gordon, would you like to catalogue my late husband's stamp collection?'

At Angelic's chateaux I found rooms full of dust covered stamp albums. For six weeks, I worked on those albums. We became more than just friends but the idyllic holiday romance came to an abrupt end. Not my fault her family were not happy. One Sunday morning four of them arrived unannounced. They dumped me in a nearby village without thanks or gratitude for my unpaid work. At a pavement café, I began a conversation with the owner, Bertrand Chevalier. His wife and daughter had left him. He could not manage the café single handed. I offered my services. What had I to lose? Yes, I lied about my experience but under the circumstances I figured it could not be my fault.

I learned to cook a few specialities and help out. All fine until Bertrand's daughter, Monique, returned. One night Monique and I fooled around, drunk on homemade pear brandy. Not my fault. She started it. Bertrand found us and tried to finish it with a meat cleaver with threats to chop off pieces of my anatomy. Monique calmed him. I am still here with Monique. Bertrand died of a heart attack two weeks ago. Not my fault. Monique is pregnant. That's all my fault with a little help from the pear brandy.

Curl Up And Die
Alison Wassell

GRAN RUINED MY life with a hairdo. I had been growing my hair for years in preparation for my escape. I needed it to run my fingers through, to toss back, to twist enticingly around my finger. I planned to be "The Girl With The Hair". I had the grades for university and my bags had been packed since August.

June gazed sadly at my reflection. 'Long and straight isn't doing you any favours, Pet. It's very lank. Oily too.'

I looked down at my lap, wondering whether to apologise.

'Are you thinking of a perm, June? Give it some body?' Gran tapped her enormous handbag. 'No expense spared. She deserves it.'

I began to picture Pre-Raphaelite waves, or a mass of untameable curls. I could live with either of those. June patted my shoulders, then rubbed her hands in anticipation.

'Don't worry, love. Those college boys won't be able to keep their hands off you.'

Gran snorted. 'She's not had a boyfriend yet.'

The salon fell silent as I was led off to be shampooed, imagining the word 'virgin' tattooed on my forehead.

When I returned Gran had been joined by a Greek chorus of pensioners, all with their handbags balanced on their knees.

'Is that her? I always pictured her petite like you, Betty.' Gran said I took after Dad's side of the family, who were big boned.

June brandished her scissors and I understood that there would be no Pre-Raphaelite waves.

I had stuffed my glasses into my cardigan pocket and I was glad of the fuzziness my world had taken on. Panic stricken, I sank into a dreamlike state, only vaguely aware of the voices, and the snipping of hair.

'What's she going to study?'

'Literature and Linguistics, or summat.'

"Or summat" was what Gran tacked on to the end of a sentence when she didn't understand something and had no wish to be enlightened.

'She's not very talkative, is she?'

'She'll have to come out of her shell, once she's there.'

In my befuddled state I mused that a snail without its shell was a slug. Who wanted to be a slug?

After the cutting came rollers and chemicals, a plastic shower cap and a kitchen timer, more shampooing, rollers, the kind of hair dryer you sat under.

'Ooh, Betty, she's the image of you.'

I replaced my glasses and looked in the mirror. June stood back to admire her handiwork. My head was a mass of short tight curls. There was malevolence in Gran's smile. Gran, who had passed the scholarship exam for the grammar school but not been allowed to go. She knew I wasn't brave enough to be "The One With The Pensioner's Perm".

I went to bed for the three years it would have taken to gain a degree. When I finally surfaced my hair had grown wild and out of control. But the moment to escape had somehow passed. Life seldom works out the way you plan it.

Options for the Ridiculously Poor

Ian Tucker

'FOR SOMEONE OF my talents, I am ridiculously poor,' said Bethan from the chaise longue. 'It's boring.'

Janis simpered uncertainly and shifted her bony buttocks on the upright chair. Purposeful footsteps sounded from the hall.

'Gary!' yelled Bethan.

Gary's hand paused on the front door handle. He couldn't pretend not to have heard.

'Gary! How can I make money?'

Some unacceptable thoughts passed across Gary's mind. He resisted the temptation and selected a neutral answer. 'Try selling something?'

'Like what? I have no morals and no qualms. However, I am not prepared to wait, obey instructions or break a sweat.' Bethan examined her nails and waited expectantly.

Janis shifted her bottom again and there was no sound from the hall.

'Which would make me more money?' yelled Bethan when the silence had become too long. 'Cigarettes, booze, weapons or drugs?'

'Try something aspirational,' said Gary, still in the hall. 'People buy things to make them feel good.' There was no immediate response, so he seized his chance and left. The best thing about his job was that it got him out of the house.

Bethan swung her fluffy-socked feet onto the floor and stared at Janis. 'What do stupid people aspire to?'

'Stupid people?' said Janis.

'Yes – ideally, *rich* stupid people?'

'I don't know.'

'Good point. Stupid people don't know what they want.' Bethan stroked her chin as if it was covered in gender-improbable stubble. Her forehead was lined with exertion and her nose twitched like a scavenging beast sensing carrion.

Silence fell.

Janis fiddled with her cuffs. Nothing she could say was going to make things better. She picked up a glamour magazine and tried to look like she was reading it.

'Wonder make-up,' said Bethan. 'Miracle hair cream to make your coif bounce. Slinky lingerie which rustles at a frequency irresistible to men. Luminous nail varnish so nobody notices your face. Instant fitness crisps in a range of flavours. Ice cream that makes you thinner.'

Janis blushed. In a moment of panic, she'd admitted to Bethan that ice cream gave her wind. She'd been waiting for the teasing ever since. So far Bethan had merely mentioned ice cream as often as possible. The unspoken ridicule was somehow worse than overt teasing.

'That last one might work,' said Bethan jumping up and pacing around the room. 'Do you think we could make cheap ice cream and claim it made you thinner? As part of a calorie-controlled diet, of course.'

'I don't know how to make ice cream,' said Janis.

'No, you wouldn't. Unfortunately, neither do I. And it sounds like effort.'

Bethan continued pacing. Janis shifted uncomfortably again

and went back to staring at an article on the resurgence of snoods. She imagined that it must have been like this in the Blitz, waiting for a bomb.

'Although,' said Bethan, her lip curling demonically, 'you always feel thinner when you've just farted so maybe there is something in it.'

Janis crossed her legs and hunched her shoulders. Bethan was unbearable in this kind of mood. It wasn't fair. Not that Bethan was ever fair.

'Maybe you should get a job,' muttered Janis, without looking up from the magazine. 'Co-op wants a sales agent.'

'Sales agent! No way I'm doing checkout...' Bethan had a distant look and the outburst faded. She stopped pacing. Janis looked up from the magazine nervously. There was nothing worse than Bethan having an idea.

'*Fart Yourself Thinner!*' announced Bethan, basking in a glow of inspiration.

Janis furrowed her brow in confusion.

A KEY TURNED in the lock and purposeful footsteps sounded from the hall.

'Gary!' yelled Bethan. The steps stopped.

'Gary! What makes you fart?'

There was a long pause. Gary was weighing up the least disastrous answer.

'Beans?' he said.

'We've got beans, oats, sprouts, cabbage, fizzy drinks, cake, cream, plums, caffeine, broccoli, artificial sweetener, laughing hysterically and ice cream.'

'Okay,' said Gary. He waited but no further enquiries were made so he crept away to his bedroom.

Bethan grinned smugly. Her plans were laid out all over the room on sheets of Janis' floral writing paper. Modesty aside, they were genius.

She clapped her hands and brought the meeting, that is to say Janis, to order. 'Right. Listen up. We have a concept – burn off those extra pounds in the form of exhaust gases. We have personal experience – who hasn't felt their waist band loosen after letting one rip? We have some spurious science – fat is made of carbon and hydrogen and most people think farts are methane which is also carbon and hydrogen, so it can't be hard to change one into the other. We have testimonials from a dozen names chosen randomly from the phone book. We have a menu sheet – two weeks of dinners to make you fart constantly. There is a list of magazines to advertise in whose readership is composed of vain imbeciles. And best of all, we have an inspired marketing strapline. All we need is some photos – you'll have to start eating cakes.'

'What?' said Janis, who was assessing the rights and wrongs of their day's work.

'We need before and after shots. We can do the after shots now because you're convincingly thin. But you'll need to bulk up for the before shots.'

'But wouldn't I have to do the diet and I'm not sure it would actually work.'

'Of course not. I can't wait for you to bulk up, take the shots and then hope you'll actually lose the spare pounds again. That would take ages and you might remain a heffalump for good. We have to seize the moment – I want an extra two stone by the end of next week. Five meals a day and extra desserts should do it. And try to fart a lot – a few audible guffs will help the video.'

'Video?'

'Yes. Obviously we'll have to film it backwards – you start by saying how happy you are with how quickly the diet worked and how athletic and energetic you feel. Then every day as you're putting on the pounds you say how well it's working until in a week's time, when you look like a hippo, you announce you are about to start the diet and are full of hope.'

'Where are you going to show this video?'

'I was thinking of the cinema – you know, at the beginning when there's sometimes a toe-curling description of the local curry house. And YouTube, of course. Also – I think you should make a point of saying that, although you are farting a lot – it only happens when you're not at work and it's a special sort of fart which never smells.'

'But I don't go to work.'

'They don't need to know that. Our victims… clients will want to believe the diet is followed by high-flying professionals. Stop making unnecessary objections. We need to go shopping for cabbagey vegetables and yoghurt – but first…'

Bethan took out her camera. 'Try to look like you've rediscovered your libido.'

BETHAN NODDED AT her laptop with satisfaction. The website was bright, appealing and had a dominating banner reading "Dr Bethan's Miracle Diet." A stylised pink cloud underneath said: "Fart Yourself Thinner!"

It was remarkable what you could do, really. That is, it was remarkable what Bethan's niece could do with a keyboard and some artistic guidance. Bethan had had to promise to take the girl to some taste-draining musical by way of incentive. However, that horror could be delayed almost indefinitely.

Janis was lying on the chaise longue surrounded by cupcakes with a video camera trained on her. She'd stopped whining after the first few days and once she'd passed the twelve stone mark had become quite compliant. She was staring at the alarm clock which rang every half hour to prompt her to eat another cake. There was a pleasant, if abnormal, curviness to her figure. As if she'd gone from Lowry to Rubens.

'Janis,' said Bethan, skimming through the long list of glowing comments she'd uploaded onto the public forum. 'I think we are ready for launch.'

'But I've only just finished my second breakfast and it's not even 11 o'clock.'

'Launch. Not Lunch. Only the financial niceties to go and then we're on the market.'

Purposeful footsteps sounded from the hall.

'Gary!' yelled Bethan, 'how much would you pay to be slim and attractive?'

Gary glanced at his waistline, which narrowed between hips and ribs. He considered objecting to the question but didn't want to delay getting to Rugby training.

'A fiver?' he said. He didn't really know why anyone would pay for diet guidance. Surely you just ate less, didn't you? That should save you money.

As no challenge came back, Gary assumed his answer was acceptable and swung his bootbag onto his shoulder and departed.

Bethan was counting on her fingers.

'So. Gary would pay five pounds,' she told Janis who was finding it very easy to fart for the camera. 'But he is already thin, so we should start by doubling that. And he is a man and they don't care what they look like, so we should double it again. And we don't want to appear cheap, so double it again.'

'Forty pounds sounds a bit steep,' said Janis.

'Quite right. Thirty-nine pounds ninety-nine pence, it is. A bargain when you think of what you get for your money.'

'Really?'

'Yes,' said Bethan, somewhat affronted. 'Access to our password-protected member's zone; three inspirational videos from our CEO and fa(r)t-loss expert – me; tasty daily menu sheets including drinks and desert; a party pack including branded badge, pencil and balloon; invitations, at some future date, to fa(r)t camps in exciting places like Launceston sands; assistance with setting up local members' support groups – provided someone organises and hosts them in your area; a very long and impenetrable essay by me on how it works; some pictures of fat and thin celebrities whose purpose is not entirely clear; a complementary but strictly unnecessary exercise regime; money off vouchers if you introduce a friend and advice on where to buy ingredients – which mostly suggests local supermarkets and grocers. All that! Not to mention the heart-tugging video diary of how awful your life was and how you've shed … how much is it now?'

'I've put on thirty-three pounds,' said Janis, proudly.

'Exactly – people won't believe the transformation. You must be delighted.'

'What happens when people try your diet and it doesn't work?' asked Janis.

'Doesn't work! How dare you? I have great confidence that it will work. Anyone who spends all day feeling bloated and is faced with a meal of Brussel sprouts in cream cheese is going to lose their appetite. They may even go for long walks just to ease the pain in their guts. The pounds will simply drop off!'

The concluding bars of Del Amitri's *Nothing Ever Happens* filled the empty room. A key turned in the front door and the presenter on Tilebury radio cantered through the names of song and artist. Gary stepped into the hall.

'And now, we're joined by renowned weight loss expert, Dr Bethan Lovelady-Slimme, who's going to get us all fit and thin for those holiday bikini shots. So, Bethan, is it true you actually met Vladimir Putin?'

Gary paused in the hall as Bethan's voice came over the airwaves.

'He's sought out my advice a few times. It's hard to keep in shape to wrestle bears, you know, when you're over sixty and go to regular state banquets. He swears by my fa(r)t loss tips although, like many eastern Europeans, from a strictly professional perspective he overdoes the cabbage.'

'But, how did you…'

'…and he was kind enough to recommend me to Barrack Obama who, as I'm sure you noticed, was beginning to podge out towards the end of his stint as president. Before I got him on the ice cream and fizzy lager of course.'

'Is it just world leaders who've followed your advice?'

'No, Dr Bethan's Miracle Fa(r)t Loss Diet is an open secret in Hollywood and, particularly, Bollywood. Not to mention Soliwood – the West-Midlands' very own glamourous filmmaking hub. Secrets are secrets, so I'll just mention a few names: Madonna, Fred and George Weasley from Harry Potter, Michelle Pfeiffer, Zsa Zsa Gabor, the entire cast of King Kong other than the monkey, Adil Ray, Judi Dench, Buzz Lightyear, Tony Hancock, Lemar.'

'…and does it really work…'

Gary managed to switch off the radio before hearing Bethan's answer. He went to the kitchen to make a sandwich and come to terms with the world in which he was living.

'A TRIUMPH,' SAID Bethan, striding up and down the rug.

'We've had three thousand hits on the website today alone,' said Janis, who was getting worried by how many times her video had been watched on Youtube. 'Someone even recognised me in the street. I had to pretend to be my own fat twin who hadn't done the diet.'

'Sales?'

Janis' voice wavered, 'Yes. We've had a thousand pounds in, people are actually paying us. Although I'm not sure...'

'We should improve our social responsibility,' interrupted Bethan. 'Post something about carbon offsetting. And say we sponsor the Young Sprouts Campaign for feeble children.'

'But...'

Running footsteps came from the staircase.

'Gary!' yelled Bethan, 'do you know any dodgy accountants who can invest my money in tax havens?'

'No,' called Gary who had adopted an avoidance tactic. 'Gotta go.' Seconds later he was through the door and into the street where he was able to slow to a more relaxed pace.

'But there's this professor who's popped up. He's saying the diet is a con,' said Janis.

'Aha! Yes! Professor Kahn. Fancy a biscuit?'

'No thanks, I've rather gone off snacks. This guy's publishing articles all over the place and has written to medical magazines and diet forums and all sorts. He's calling you a charlatan.'

'How dare he say such things?'

'Largely on the basis that you have no qualifications or background, aren't actually a doctor and your claims are vague and dubious.'

'Hmmm. Fair enough. Although how much do you really need to know? It's only a diet after all.'

'But he'll ruin everything.'

'How little you understand, you overinflated lady-balloon,'

said Bethan, making a wafting gesture and shrugging her shoulders. 'This will be brilliant for sales. A real life professor is making my product controversial and there's nothing like controversy for profile raising. Maybe we should sue him for defamation and start spreading stories that his own diet failed and he had to resort to liposuction in a secretive Swiss clinic.'

'But if we accuse him of lying, people will ask us for evidence of our own approach.'

'Au contraire mon frere,' said Bethan, 'classic distraction technique. Accuse your enemy of whatever they accuse you of. Worked for Stalin, it'll work for us.'

'But Stalin was...'

'Enough, Janis. I'm not sure I care enough. I'll probably just rise above it all and have a little nap.'

'WE'VE HAD SOME complaints,' said Janis.

'How? I told you to publish a fake email address and not to give out a phone number or postal address. We should only be contactable through the online shop and then only for purchases,' said Bethan, who was sending inflammatory texts on Gary's smartphone.

'There's a message board on the website. It's full of nasty things.'

'Follicles! Just delete them. Control the medium, control the message. Post some stinging vitriol from real people about the incompetence of so-called experts and how the diet is proving the nay-sayers and haters wrong.'

'But don't we need some real facts to back it up?'

'No-one believes real facts, Janis, they're too complicated. People prefer bold inaccuracies they wish were true. We should probably bump up the material on the website about the diet's preventative effect on small pox, leprosy and tuberculosis.'

'Haven't those all been eradicated?'

'Perhaps. But they still sound scary. And we can claim that no users of my diet have suffered from them. I don't have time for all this. Where's Gary?'

'Haven't seen him for days. He leaves before I get up and comes back when I'm in bed. I'm not sleeping well because of the indigestion.'

'Slacker.'

'Once you delete all the complaints, the message board is really weird. There are loads of positive comments and I didn't post them all,' said Janis, whose features had reappeared sufficiently from under the fat to display confusion.

'Maybe it works after all,' said Bethan, who was staring out the window. Something feral had appeared behind her eyes and a manic smile was taking over her face.

'Do you think we could use this to prove Professor Kahn wrong?' asked Janis.

'Who cares? I've had enough anyway. Time to close the whole thing down.'

Janis' mouth fell open. 'But you can't do that!' she said. 'Not now. There are people out there who want to buy things from us. We can't let them down.'

'Of course we can. I didn't do all this just to answer moany questions from idiots, bandy words with professors and organise fart-athons.'

'Didn't you?'

'No. The whole thing lacks social worth. I deserve a better legacy. And I've had a much better idea.'

Janis gaped. 'But all that effort, and all those cupcakes.'

'It's boring and my other idea is so much better. It will take the internet of things, wearable technology and instant communications to an unparalleled new level of personal relevance. It'll make me famous. And everyone will love it – even Gary.'

Janis almost started hyperventilating. 'What is it?' she was just brave enough to ask.

'This is the big one, Janis, my time has come.'

Janis couldn't speak. She just nodded.

Bethan swelled her chest and opened her arms wide. Janis cringed.

'*Smart-pants*,' said Bethan. 'A *new era of crotch communications*. Just tell me that won't sell.'

Janis winced.

Thou Shalt Not Kill
Bettina Daniel

1

THE PLAN WAS simple and we pulled it off except for killing the other guy. We would exit the plane right behind the target; his shaved head was easy to follow. Jack would throw the smoke bomb, I would take the target out.

We didn't count on the target being ready for us. As I shot him, he got off two shots himself. One hit Jack, one hit the guy next to me. He fell against the wall of the jetway, gazing at my gun. Then he raised his eyes to mine and stared.

'Theresa,' he said, slowly and carefully.

I shot him in the stomach, three times. Little bits of flesh were warm on my arm.

We ran. Jack was hurt. Sirens were going off. There were ambulances at the taxi stand.

'He's hurt, get us out of here,' I yelled in French to the EMTs in the first one. They strapped Jack in and we raced away, alarm blaring.

Jack was pale but conscious.

'What's that?' he mouthed, gesturing with his good arm to the backpack at my feet.

I looked at it for the first time. I had just grabbed it.

It's the other guy's backpack,' I answered.

2

JACK GOT A bed right away. A woman doctor examined and said he would need immediate surgery.

'Will he die?'

'We'll all die. He'll do it sooner if he doesn't have surgery. Does he consent?'

Jack looked at me wordlessly.

'We need a decision here.'

I hesitated. This wasn't protocol. 'Yes,' I finally said, not taking my eyes off Jack.

She nodded to two orderlies – barked 'Room 6!' – and moved on.

I sat next to Jack's empty, curtained-off bed as the ward filled up with mutters and wails. After what seemed like an hour, I looked down at the three bags – mine, Jack's, and the other guy's.

I took Jack's bag first. He always followed protocol. So I knew what to expect, and it was all there. Clothes and ordinary toiletries. Things that looked like toiletries but were actually weapons. The ditty bag with passports sewn inside the foam lining. Everything would look normal unless you knew.

There was also a card full of smiley faces and Xs and Os and initials. I guess Jack thought that was anonymous enough. I started to destroy it – then I changed my mind.

When you're in a broken country, you see things you can't imagine back home. You become a patriot like starving people become food lovers. For some people, that connects with family. Back in the Army, Jack would say, 'I have three sisters. Guys here don't let their sisters go to school.' Family made Jack proud, even when he was just training. 'Uncle Jack drives trucks around the desert,' he'd say to the kids.

If you don't have family, you do it for your buddies. You've burrowed so far into this world that ordinary people seem – well, useless. But you'd do anything for your buddies.

Like I was doing in that Marseilles hospital for Jack.

3

SILENCE SETTLED. I decided to see what was in the other guy's bag. Clothes and hiking gear—expensive. Camera in fancy padded cases. Guide books for Spain, and a little book to write in, halfway filled up already. No wallet – that would have been in his back pocket. Same with his phone.

The bag itself was covered with blood and dust. I cleaned it with the sanitized wipes in the room. I washed and put on clothes from the other guy's bag. They fit. The shirt had three little stains under the arm—like tiny little splashes of something that would never wash out—but no one would get close enough to me to see them.

I kept the guidebooks and a few other things. There was a bin where they'd put Jack's clothes after they cut them off to look at his wound—I put my empty bag and clothes underneath. Cleaning the other guy's bag once more I found a small card with handwriting on it: *Joe OWEN* and a phone number, and: *In emergency contact Theresa OWEN*, and another number. I dipped it in water and ate it.

IT WAS HOURS before Jack came back.

The doctor said: 'He'll live – we've given him a sleeping drug,' and left.

I let myself doze, hugging the other guy's bag, now mine.

4

PROTOCOL WAS THAT we'd been paid half in advance. The other half would be wired to a separate account after the client was satisfied that the target had been wiped. We would receive a text message, either containing further instructions (bad) or the account number (good).

I was dozing when the text came through. It was a number. I went to work. The inside of his left upper arm was the place I'd decided on. His skin was taut there—Jack was a compulsive lifter—and the job went fast. With luck no one would see but him. There would be a little pain, like with all new tattoos, but maybe he would assume it was related to his injuries, or be so drugged up he wouldn't notice. When he did, he'd know. And he'd be set for life.

The last thing to do was to take his phone and all his passports but one. I picked one of the current spares—completely made up. Jack was a new man.

5

I HAD TO get to this place St Jean Pied de Port. The sun was just coming up when I boarded the city bus at the hospital, with people coming off the night shift, and I rode it to the end of the line. It took two changes to get to St Jean.

The trip to Toulouse was quiet. That ended once I changed at Bayonne. Pilgrims. The first were Germans who had expensive equipment like mine and seemed to know where they were going. At that point I began to think about my own identity, because I had to decide what language to say "I don't speak German" in, if the need arose. But it didn't. I got on the bus, back window seat, and closed my eyes. When I woke up we were on a highway, and when I woke up again we were in country.

Time to think. Need to choose. I had an assortment of faces in the foam lining of my ditty bag, and thought about which to use. I could be convincing in French (Canadian accent) or Portuguese (Rhode Island accent). I decided on Portuguese for now, put that passport in an accessible zippered pocket, and went back to sleep. I hadn't slept much for weeks.

At St Jean's there were lots of people with hiking sticks they weren't sure what to do with, and an air of subdued excitement. The whole town seemed to be tourist restaurants and hostels. I knew from the book what the hostels were like—not enough privacy. Right now I needed to stay out of sight for a month or two, and hope the investigations would focus on people in France—which I would leave, on foot, the next day.

6

ON DAY 1 of the Camino you go up the Pyrenees on the French side. If you're fast, you can go all the way to the Spanish border and cross it on the morning of the second day. If you're slow, you cross it in the afternoon. There weren't supposed to be passport checks between EU countries, but you never knew. Afternoon shifts are busier, and better for these things than morning, so I set my pace with the slower walkers. People mixed groups, and there were other solo travelers like me.

At the first café bar most of them went inside. I was prepared to blow on by, but then realized my best tactic was to stay with the crowd, and do what they did. So I sipped my coffee, and smoked. I even put my bag on the other chair, which was against protocol and felt odd, but would keep anyone from asking to join me.

The second day of the trip was much the same. After lunch

we came to the border: an old tin sign that said "Spain." But there was, as I'd feared, a temporary checkpoint: a folding desk with a truck nearby. The agents looked annoyed. I suddenly realized that I would be asked why, if I'm Portuguese, I was coming on the French trail rather than the Portuguese. I got out of the line, went to the toilet, shut the door, put the Portuguese passport back in the lining, and dug out an old American one. Not just an old one – the original one, with the name I was born with. I would show the passport that I hadn't used since I first left the US. I edged up the line. The agent looked at his watch and shouted something about a break to the guy at the next station. He looked perfunctorily at the passport of the woman in front of me, and then at mine, saying "Welcome to Spain" in an absent tone before turning his station over to the agent in the next shift, who examined the passport behind me in detail. I stepped out of France and into Spain.

7

THAT AFTERNOON IT got hot. Coffees became beers, complaints about blisters started. This was most days—brisk mornings, hot afternoons. People who had done the Camino before also warned of sudden rain. I reverted to Portuguese, and used that passport to check in to hotels.

Days went by when I saw no one other than pilgrims on the trail and people working the café bars and hotels. Some of the places we stayed were no more than wide spots in the road. If there were police stations, I didn't see them, although friendly looking men with "Gardia Civil" vests sometimes loitered at the coffee counters, bantering with the staff and reading the local papers, which were in Galician dialect. Galician dialect is enough like Portuguese for me to understand, although it seemed like I was reading something very old.

Some days we didn't see a car the whole day. We saw more cows than people.

I'd toyed with the idea of staying at a hotel for two nights, and tried it once, but after being asked over and over by the hotel and café people if I was all right, realized that was unusual and would attract attention. So I let myself be carried on the stream of pilgrims. They chatted, but respected people who didn't want to chat. These were not wary people. I was becoming less wary myself.

8

THEN WE REACHED the mesa – long, flat fields without trees or bushes, where the few buildings could be spotted a long way off. I realized here how reassured I had been to have a rocky, wooded landscape around me. Like everyone else in my profession, I'd been trained as a survivalist, and (at least in theory) could disappear into the woods and sustain myself off the human grid. Like jumping out of a perfectly good airplane, or testing your body armor – these things gave us the confidence to think that we were superhuman. The mesa landscape stripped this feeling away for me—and we'd be walking it for days.

That's when the rain came. It rumbled on the first morning and broke by lunch. By the time we stepped back out on the trail, it was coming down hard. Everyone had their ponchos on, like a parade of hunchbacks. For days we shuffled through the wet.

There were fewer café bars on this stretch, so we all had our dry stops and warm drinks together. One day it was a small bar and we filled up every chair and every bench. The people behind the bar kept the coffees coming. We heard the rain pick up and then thunder and wind. The owner replied with a firm headshake and pursed lips when one of the Americans asked him something. As the noise picked up again, two more people entered—two of the German women I'd first encountered on the bus. One was quiet, the other a little friendlier, both with an air of competence. The only places to sit were on the bench where the person next to me and I had put our bags. We moved them and the women sat down. The one next to me, the quiet one, gave me a kind smile, then got up to get coffees. As she handed one to her companion, I saw that they were a couple.

The conversation was at first animated, as everyone asked all the usual questions—where did you start, when, how far did you come today—and then died down. It was getting humid. The woman next to me leaned back and closed her eyes. As she relaxed her body, her legs shifted position and her thigh touched mine. She didn't seem to notice, but I did. It was the first human flesh I had touched in weeks. It was warm.

That night, when I got in bed, I worked myself violently, imagining the two of them in bed. Then I took the other guy's notebook out of the backpack and began to read it.

Unhappy couples always sound alike. It's all me, me, me. Maybe I'm bitter. Anyway, Joe, his name was Joe, complained a lot about his wife, Theresa. But he also seemed curious about her and confused by what she wanted. I looked at the photo—she was pretty, in a chubby way. I wondered what he didn't understand.

As I read on, I realized that Joe had been sleeping with someone else—her best friend, Linda. Theresa had found out. Joe had apologized, repented, swore never again. She threw him out anyway, and didn't let him see the kids. I wondered how old the kids were and put the book down. That night I dreamed of Quebec and Rhode Island.

9

WE HAD THREE more days on the Mesa. The first two continued rainy, and all the conversations were all about rain, wet socks, and blisters. Then the last day came, bright and cloudless. And lots of mud. On we trudged.

Here was where I realized that it wasn't just one particular group of pilgrims that I had traveled with for the three weeks. Whether I slowed down or sped up, there were pilgrims ahead of us and behind us, a stream, soon to be a river in the summertime, down to a trickle in the winter, but never really beginning or ending. I was immersed in that stream.

The town after the mesa was Sarria – where people start who want to make a short pilgrimage. There are a lot of them, and that meant more cops, but they seemed more focused on pickpockets than anything else.

And pickpocketing was exactly what I had in mind. I knew the best way to replenish my cash would be to relieve one of these new pilgrims of their Euros. Jetlagged and drunk is a good combination for this, so I went to a bar.

The operation was simple. A large group of people, drinking and playing darts. Women had left their little purses all over. It was too easy to stop at one, so I got two, extracted the cash, and left the purses where they'd be easily found. I was 700 Euros richer, so pleased with myself that I let myself have one more drink than usual.

10

IT WAS IN Melide two days later that I had my first bad moment. I was at breakfast. Two American guys came down. They were dressed in ordinary clothes and shoes. And they weren't acting like pilgrims. They were tense.

The two guys sat behind me, so I couldn't catch everything they said. Then I heard the word that made my skin tighten.

'Theresa.'

'What about her?'

'She's in a bad way.'

'Well of course. Her husband's shagging her best friend. She's pissed.'

'No, I mean she's worried. Really worried.'

'Well, what the fuck would we be here for if she wasn't?'

'We're here to find him. To talk to him. To make sure he takes care of her and the kids and doesn't just wander off with her money.'

'And ours.'

'Ours, sure, yeah.'

Silence for a while as they ate and went back for more. I pretended to finish the news and turned to the puzzles.

'Family businesses. More trouble'n they're worth. I shoulda gone to work for…. I dunno, the phone company.'

'Yeah, well, ya didn't, so here we are.'

'Are we sure he's here?'

'He's supposed to be in this hotel. Reservation for last night. He should be at breakfast, right now.'

'He didn't check in. Didn't at the last one either.'

'You got a better idea?'

Silence.

'How did Theresa find out?'

'The same way she found out about the other thing. Credit card bill. It went to his office. Dumb fuck left it in his pocket. It was sitting there until she went through his suits three days ago.'

'What else do we know?'

'Hotel here, hotels for the last two weeks, flight to Marseilles before that. Hotels from here to Santiago. Three nights there. Flight back to JFK.'

'Did he bring the broad here?'

'Nope – all singles. And just one airplane ticket. Round trip.'

'Funny place to get away.'

'It's religious, kind of.'

'You mean he's sorry?'

'If I had Theresa on my ass, I'd be sorry. Teresa cuts and takes the kids, Linda goes back to her boyfriend, we throw him out of the business – yeah, I'd be real sorry if I was Joe.'

'So whadda we do now?'

'We wait, you sorry schmuck. And we hope Joe turns up, all cooperative. And we bring him back and hand him over to Theresa.'

'Poor Theresa. She deserves better.'

'Poor Theresa? She's not your sister! Always whining, always wanting something…'

More silence.

'So we just wait for Joe to saunter in, just like that? What's he gonna wear? What if he's in some kind of disguise?'

'You watch too many movies. He's gonna wear what everyone here wears – hiking clothes. Theresa says he bought a bunch of them. And some fancy backpack.'

'Fancy – how?'

'How the fuck do I know? She just said fancy.'

'What color?'

'What color, the man wants to know. What if I said blue?'

I tried not to look at my blue backpack.

'Okay, okay. I'm just trying to find Joe.'

'I'm just thinking what I'll do to him when I find him.'

I got up, looking as casual as I could, and walked out.

My first instinct was to run, but that made no sense. These

guys clearly had no idea who I was. They were looking for Joe. This meant that the protocol worked, as it usually did: my three shots to Joe's stomach with the exploding bullets had destroyed his phone and wallet completely. They thought he was still alive. I replayed the moment. His stare. "Theresa." The three shots. His warm flesh on my arm.

11

I STARTED TO walk. It was a day like any other—brisk but would be hot later, dry but would rain later, pilgrims disappearing and reappearing, café bars in the middle of the woods. My mind was playing out options.

The guys back at the hotel had Joe's itinerary. They were looking for him but didn't seem to have involved the police. They had nothing on me. But eventually the police would get involved, and link the body at Marseilles with the missing American man. And eventually they would think of the Camino.

It was a matter of complete cleanliness: wiping clean every single sign of myself. I was doing this every day. All my transactions, even hotels, were cash. Everything I had was in my one backpack. Every morning I put everything from my hotel room back into that pack and moved on. I was moving through the Camino like a ghost.

Once I left the Camino, an all-cash life would attract attention. Eventually I could establish a credit card account and pay it off with money from the job. There was plenty. But then I'd be traceable again—the police had ways of finding accounts with suspicious patterns. I could leave Spain—for Portugal, maybe—but eventually that would pose the same problems. A country with a big cash economy—Greece or maybe Italy—might work. Best would be a place without extradition treaties. We all knew the list. But I wasn't ready for that yet.

FOR NOW, I was pretty safe. As long as I stayed alone on the Camino, erasing myself as I went along.

12

PRETTY SAFE. THAT'S different from safe, and once you start thinking that way, everything changes. You have to think about what's behind you as well as what's in front of you. You want eyes in the back of your head—or sunglasses with rear view mirrors, which I happened to have. This made me feel safe, but it also made me crazy. I had come to like the solitude of the green trails, when I could lose other pilgrims by speeding up or slowing down. The glasses meant that when I speeded up I could watch them recede from view. This was good, but it made me walk even faster, and see other pilgrims. If I slowed down, I could lose the current batch, but there were always some behind me. It wasn't like being chased, exactly but it made me feel crowded, even out there in the middle of nowhere.

I tried to duck the two American guys. But you can't walk backwards on the Camino—the whole thing is just one long one-way street. Even if I avoided their hotels I would see them at restaurants and café bars, bickering and grumbling. Everyone complained about blisters, and they were no exception. They just did it more loudly than everyone else. It was like traveling with embarrassing relatives.

'Damn! Another blister!'

'You don't have to take your socks off in the middle of the restaurant.'

'This is not a restaurant. It's the outdoors, for chrissakes.'

'Still. You think the ladies like to eat their sandwiches looking at your ugly feet?'

This with a leer at the two German women at the next table, trying their best to ignore them.

'I bet they got blisters too.'

'Yeah, well maybe they're too classy to show them to God and everybody.'

One German raised an eyebrow to the other and stifled a smile.

As the trail took us closer to Santiago, their patience for walking gave way completely.

'Look, there are goddamn taxis everywhere. Enough with the walking. We're not gonna find Joe hiding out here in the woods behind a tree. He's gonna go to the first big city and scram.'

'Scram? Scram where?'

'Somewhere he can – I dunno, disappear.'

'With what?'

'All the money in their joint accounts, you asshole.'

'Oh, like Theresa hasn't thought of that already? And blocked them?'

'Theresa's dumb as a post. She wouldn't have the first idea how to do that.'

'You shouldn't talk about your sister that way.'

'What, you're going soft on Theresa? Is that why you're out here?'

'I'm here to find Joe! Because he's part of the family business! And he might be in trouble.'

'OK, Batman. You find him. I'm gonna get in that taxi. See you in Santiago.'

13

WALKING INTO SANTIAGO, the trails stopped being all about

pilgrims and more about city life. It meant I had choices to make in order to stay hidden.

The best place for that in Santiago is the cathedral. There were long lines to get in. The security men were professionals, but they were on the lookout for terrorists. They didn't give me a second glance.

Inside it was as crowded as a soccer stadium. A brass band was playing, a little off key. An army band, in their camos. A group of men in long robes walked down the aisle, holding gold things. They moved slowly up the steps to the platform in the middle, which was partly blocked from view by a large carved wall of pillars, straight and twisted and painted in gold. The gold was bright in some places but mostly smudged. On the top were huge statues of baby angels with pink skin and large eyes, perched on the edge of the arches, little fat arms reaching out.

The music changed. A stir was sounding in the church and people were looking up and pointing, not at the angels or the carvings, but straight up. There was a ceiling higher than the rest, like the inside of a bowl, with stone supports that met in the middle. Hung between two of the stone supports was a simple metal pulley, and hanging from it by a thick rope was a huge metal object, about six feet high and four feet wide, round, with carving like everything else and four large handles. People were pulling out their cellphones and taking pictures. I looked in my guidebook – this thing was called a *thurible*, and it had been used for centuries as an incense burner, to cover the smell of unwashed pilgrims.

As I looked, the *thurible* jerked upward and then came slowly downward. Six large men in red robes were holding onto six ropes with knots in them, all joined to one thick rope that went up to the pulley, coiled around it, and came down the other side with its load. The jerk upward came from the men unfastening their ropes. They lowered the *thurible* slowly with a hand-over-hand operation. They stopped when it was about three feet from the floor. One of the men fed it with a giant spoon and lit the contents with a candle. The five men still at the ropes raised it a few feet higher, and the sixth man gave it a shove perpendicular from the platform. It swung over the heads of the people sitting and standing – a thousand of them. As he walked unhurriedly back to his rope, the other five men lifted the *thurible* higher. Then they all gave their ropes a good tug, causing it to swing even higher in the other direction, and they all stopped it in unison by holding their ropes fast at the same time, coming together in a circle and standing on their toes. Then another good tug, and it went even higher up.

As this burning metal thing went higher and higher, I thought of a bomb. A wrecking ball. A car, out of control. Every time it went up on the other side, I could see the flames. My mouth was open.

Instinctively I looked up at the pulley. It looked old. I wondered about the connections, and the stress points, and how often they tested it. And then two things happened.

First, there was a stir behind me, and a female voice shouting, 'Joe!'

And then, from a different direction entirely – across the cathedral and far up – there was a sound of metal ripping.

The weight of the *thurible* had stressed its metal fastening, which screeched and broke. The *thurible* went out of its orbit. It careened to the other side and back to our side, up to the outstretched arms of the giant baby angel. The *thurible* crashed into it and broke it off. The deadly angel came hurtling toward me.

14

I HAD JUMPED out of the way, but all around was panic. There were, my guess was, less than ten exits for a thousand terrified people. Enforcing order would save lives.

So that's what I did. Of course that's what the guards were doing too, and my English and training helped. The important thing was to get people out of the building's few exits without a stampede.

Then I went to work on first aid, starting with the closest victim. That was a woman with thick black hair, well rounded and probably pretty when she wasn't lying in a pool of her own blood. I was applying a tourniquet on her arm when her gaze shifted slowly from my eyes to the three little stains on my shirt and back again.

Her mouth tried to work. 'Where… is… Joe?' she said, with great effort.

I could see her consciousness fighting with the blood gurgling up her throat and choking her. Her eyes looked desperate. I knew what I had to do, even if it wasn't exactly protocol.

'Theresa,' I said.

She stared at me, eyes wild, lips working pointlessly.

'Joe loves you,' I said.

Her eyes stopped fighting. She looked calm. I stayed with her until she stopped breathing.

By the time I left the cathedral, it was about nine—an hour left of sunlight. We'd worked for almost four hours. The security guys, the EMTs, the civil guards, the army guys—and me. The streets around the cathedral, usually just for pedestrians, were clogged with emergency vehicles. I walked through them unhurriedly, openly, nodding greeting to the now familiar faces of the men in uniform.

I wanted a beer, and looked for a café with a table in the sun.

Chronic

Sarah Baxter

THIS IS THE place where a girl with a pink scalp and fuzzy blonde hair screams all night as she's forced-fed tablets. I'd scream too if I kept being woken to take tablets. I can't even manage paracetamol. (Mum has to crush it into jam.) At visiting time the next morning, the doctor tells her parents that her blood's all better and she can go home. She must have been here ages because her "Get Well Soon" balloons are all wrinkly. The girl's family arrives at teatime. There's a party in the ward with a sponge cake and candles like it's a birthday. Cake slices are passed around on paper plates. Matron brings me an apple.

This is the place where Mum and Dad draw the green curtain after the doctor comes, leaving me in bed while they're on the other side. Shadow-puppet Mum stands with her face in her hands for five whole minutes. Dad's head drops and then he disappears. I tug black headphones from their hook on the wall. The radio only has one channel. I hold the headphones to my ears and listen to *Lady In Red* requested by Betty in Constable Ward recovering from a hip operation. This is the place where a boy—older than me, a thin teenager—is wheeled in on Wednesday. The nurse sticks wires on his chest attached to a heart thingy. He is here for "observations" overnight. His Dad arrives and cuffs him around the head, all jokey, telling him off. (Mum tells me later the boy electrocuted himself mucking about with his mates and his guitar. I think that sounds cool.)

This is the place where Mum drags out all the broken wheelchairs and walking frames from the bathroom. She says I should have told her I hadn't been washed for four days. Mum rushes home and returns with towels before Visiting is over. She lays them across the grey lino. She runs the water and reaches into her handbag. She brings out an unwrapped bar of Imperial Leather.

'Use this,' she says. 'You don't know where their soap's been.'

As Mum stands guard outside (the lock is broken) I lay with only my nose above water, listening to my heartbeat. I wish I had cancer. I wish I had a bad hip. I wish I was electrocuted because forever is a lot longer—it's ages. This is the place where a nurse in a blue uniform sets a kidney dish on the cabinet next to my bed. She says I have to learn this and I know she's right because this is forever. The dish contains a syringe, a tiny glass bottle of clear liquid, and an orange. The nurse pushes up her sleeve and says I can practice on her or the fruit. In the end I stick the needle right into my thigh because I'm not brave enough to hurt the nurse, or the orange.

Boys Outside

Laurence Jones

LIKE MOST TWELVE-YEAR-OLDS, Benjamin Hall worried about many things. His grandfather had died of cancer earlier that year and now his own father was collapsing beneath the weight of his loss. Where once Jacob Hall's eyes had sparkled with mischief and joy, now they were sullen and dull. Most days, Benjamin watched him lumber around their house like a zombie, adrift on medication, unblinking and dumb. As far as Benjamin was concerned, his father was no longer there, even though he was in fact quite there.

It was in spite of such misery that Benjamin's greatest adventure began. He woke one night to the sound of his parents' muffled voices reverberating up the stairs. Eventually, he gathered enough courage to venture out onto the landing, sitting beside the wooden bannister and gripping it with one hand as if he might suddenly fall. The shadows of his parents danced before him at the foot of the stairs.

'It's like staring into a well, Carrie. And all you can see at the bottom is mud and shit and stagnant water,' said Jacob.

'That's very poetic,' said Carrie. 'Very evocative.'

'I'm trying to make you understand.'

Benjamin could sense his mother holding her tongue and, when she spoke at last, her voice was tender and light. 'I understand,' she said. 'Really I do. But you have to let us in, Jacob. All of us. Whatever's going on, this isn't you anymore. Your son needs you.'

Their shadows moved closer together, heads bowed as if in silent prayer.

'I don't know what is. But I want it to stop. I really do.'

'Take him with you.'

'He's too young—'

'He's twelve years old. He's not a kid anymore. You've been telling me that for years.'

'I know what I said.'

'Then take him.'

'It's a bunch of guys drinking beer, Carrie. That's it. And the other kids, they're older than him. It's a different set of rules. They don't want a twelve-year-old hanging around—'

Benjamin felt his throat tighten and tears well up in his eyes.

'Oh come on, Jacob—'

'Seriously.'

'It'll do him good to spend some time with older kids. And what about Nicky McCormack's daughter? She's the same age.'

'Aimee?'

Benjamin wiped the tears from his eyes with the cuff of his pyjamas. He gripped the bannister tighter.

'Exactly. She's in Benjamin's year. They'll have a ball out there. The waterfalls and ravines, the campfires up on the clearings.'

'It can be dangerous.'

'Then it's a good job you'll be with him.'

Benjamin watched his father's shadow raise a hand to its forehead.

'There are bears up there—'

'God damn it, Jacob. Quit making excuses. He's your son

and he's going with you.'

His father sighed. 'Okay,' he said at last.

'Jacob?'

'What?'

'I love you.'

Benjamin watched as his parents embraced, saw them merge like molten glass then cool into something beautiful and strange. His heart and mind, however, were already quickening. The Teutonic plates of earth had just shifted. He was going on one of his father's camping trips *and* Aimee McCormack was going to be there. He crawled back to bed on his hands and knees, his smile so rigid it hurt.

***

THE NEXT MORNING, Carrie confirmed the news about the trip.

'Will you be okay?' she said.

The explosion of pure joy in Benjamin's brain nearly buckled his legs. 'Of course.'

His mother ran her fingers through his scruffy hair, kissed him on the forehead. 'He's not right yet,' she said. 'But he's trying.'

'I know that.'

'Good,' she said. 'Be safe.'

Over the next hour, Jacob packed the car up, the boot filled to bursting with camping equipment and beer slabs, and then they were gone.

It didn't seem to matter that his father barely spoke as they drove. Benjamin was buzzing with excitement, a magnificent picture show of infinite possibility swirling around his mind. He imagined he and his father sharing a beer around the campfire, the stars lit up above them, the first embers of dawn burning up across the treetops. This would be a trip to remember.

'Dad?' said Benjamin.

'What?' His father's voice was tepid as pond water.

'Are there bears out in the woods?'

Jacob looked at Benjamin as if he had suddenly gone mad. 'Of course. Do you want to go back?'

'No,' said Benjamin. 'No way. It's just I heard there were bears out there. That it was dangerous.'

Jacob sniffed and wiped his nose with the cuff of his shirt. 'We've never had a problem,' he said. 'Not in twenty years. Just be careful.'

Benjamin nodded. 'You ever see one?'

'What?'

'A bear.'

'No.'

'Never?'

'Not in fifteen years.'

'We'll be together anyway, right?'

'Sure,' said Jacob. 'Most of the time.'

Benjamin tried to ignore the awful disappointment bleeding through his veins. 'Okay,' he said.

He stared out the window as the desert rushed by.

***

FORTY-FIVE MINUTES INTO their trek to camp, Benjamin's mood became grievous. His legs were tired, his rucksack heavy, and his father was marching ahead of him at pace, dragging a trolley of beer slabs like it was the most precious cargo on earth.

'Hurry up,' he said.

'Can we stop for a minute?'

Jacob hesitated then kept on walking. 'No.'

Eventually, sun scorched desert rocks gave way to the scattered greens of the Saguaro National Park. Benjamin took a moment to stop and stare at the hills and woodlands as they walked down a steep path towards its basin. It was a majestic sight, both primitive and raw, sprawled out beneath the brightest blue sky he had even seen. Even better, a hundred yards ahead on a sparse and dusty clearing, a dozen or so middle-aged men were congregating around tents and a bonfire.

It was Bill Hudson, dressed in khaki and a camouflage cap, who noticed their approach. 'Hall,' he shouted, lumbering towards them with a beer in hand. 'It's the Hall-master!'

Before Benjamin knew what was happening, a barrage of ecstatic whoops and hollers rained down upon them. Bill grasped his arm dragged them to the centre of his father's rapturous friends. Thereafter, for a few precious minutes, squinted eyes were raised up to the scorching sun and fresh beers were sprung open with an effervescent whoosh then toasted. It felt, to Benjamin, as if he finally belonged. And, glancing over at his father's face, he saw, for the first time in a long while, the subtle curve of a smile upon his face.

Sadly, this minor interlude of joy was ripped to shreds by the arrival of Aimee McCormack, a feisty blond beauty of such epic proportions that Benjamin could barely breathe in her presence. Dressed in cut-off jeans and a Lakers t-shirt, she sat down on the other side of the circle, next to her father, and stared at the ground. And for the next twenty minutes, while a dozen fathers laughed and joked and reminisced about the wild lives they had once lived, Benjamin spent his time nervously staring anywhere he could except at Aimee's long bare legs stretched out before him.

Eventually, Aimee's dad turned and put his arm around her. 'Why don't you guys catch up with the other kids down at the creek?'

Aimee squirmed theatrically away from him. 'Dad –'

'Come on, Aimee.'

'I don't want to go anywhere.'

'Just for an hour. This is God's country. Go enjoy some of it.'

Benjamin marvelled at the complexity of her reaction. She seemed so adult, so many things at once—a slighted victim, a righteous protestor, an angry mistress. He could scarcely believe they were the same age. Aimee was, he concluded, the most remarkable girl he had ever met.

And then, without warning, she got to her feet, pulled her jeans back down the tanned skin of her thigh, and spoke.

'Come on,' she said. 'Let's go.'

It took a nudge from Jacob, a well-placed elbow in the ribs to be accurate, to make Benjamin realise she was talking to him. The circle of men fell silent and, when he finally looked up, Aimee was already halfway towards the forest trails.

'Go for it,' said Jacob.

Benjamin felt a familiar gnaw of anxiety. Something terrible awaited him in that forest. His sense for impending humiliation verged on being a superpower. The other kids would pick on him, Aimee would destroy him. His journey back to the adults would be one of utter shame and loneliness.

He felt his father's hand on his shoulder.

'Be bold,' he said.

And so Benjamin stood up, dusted himself down and started walking. There was time enough, as fallen leaves crunched beneath his feet and the pine trees loomed ever higher, for one last glance over his shoulder. He locked eyes with Jacob Hall.

'Son,' he said.

'What?' said Benjamin, desperate for a last-minute reprieve.

'Watch out for those bears.'

The other men around the campfire hollered with laughter.

Benjamin held his father's gaze just long enough to communicate a single telepathic message, a voice he could hear quite clearly in his own head. 'You son of a bitch,' it said.

***

TO HIS SURPRISE, Benjamin found great joy in his journey. Aimee's father had been quite correct: the forest was a treasure trove of unexpected delights, from the thick perfume of tree sap in the air to the way the blue sky and scattered clouds looked like a river passing above them. Indeed, it felt as if Benjamin's whole world had been flipped upside down, such was the spirit of adventure now coursing through his veins. Aimee marched ahead at first, muttering about twigs in sneakers and parties being missed back home until, eventually, she condescended to stop for him.

'We're nearly there,' she said. 'And you better man up and quickly. Tony and the others will eat you alive if you keep moping about.'

Benjamin felt his mouth dry out. 'Okay.'

They continued to walk, the forest trees becoming more disparate around them, until they came to a clearing beside a wide river, its waters sparkling white in the sunshine. There, sat on its banks, surrounded by Stussy rucksacks and empty beer cans, were Tony Dean and his merry band of miscreants. Tony looked over at them, all sharp cheekbones and fringe, and nodded.

Benjamin felt his heart sink in his chest. He turned and looked back at the forest. It felt somehow as if the trees were alive, that a hundred eyes were spying on him. Judgement was everywhere. And so he quickened his pace, drew close to Aimee's side, and prepared for the best of the worst.

***

BENJAMIN STARED AT the gun, a pristine Colt, which lay on the moss-covered rock before him like an Arthurian sword.

'Pick it up,' said Andy Hudson.

It was not that Benjamin had never seen a real gun before. He just despised them. 'Where did you get it?' he said.

'Andy's dad's got a whole case of them,' said Tony. 'We figured he wouldn't miss one for the weekend.' He walked over to the rock, picked up the gun and handed it to Benjamin. 'This is our constitutional right, my friend, to bear arms. Are you a patriot, Benjamin?'

The rest of his crew began to laugh.

'Don't be so stupid,' said a lone voice.

Benjamin turned and looked at Aimee. He tried to speak but all that came out were tiny gasps. He stared at the gun in Tony's hand. The stakes had been raised unimaginably.

'Hurry up already,' said Rufus Jenkins, the most odious of the bunch, his face glowering and impatient. 'You some kind of goddamn pussy?'

Benjamin glanced up at the five empty beer cans on the rock nearby and grasped the handle, the metal warm to the touch.

'Aim and pull the trigger, Benjamin,' said Tony. His voice was a cocktail of charm and mischief. 'For your country.'

'Don't you dare,' said Aimee. 'Don't you dare. Do you hear me?'

'Take them out, man,' said Rufus.

Benjamin felt sweat trickling down his brow. He looked down at the gun in his clammy hand then clicked the safety catch and raised it towards the targets. The memory of his father and friends laughing flashed before his eyes. He eased his finger against the trigger.

The next few moments were a cacophony of gunfire and terrified screams. Benjamin's act of killing was most shocking perhaps because no one expected it from him. His shots were expertly fired, the lead bullets tearing and cauterising flesh with each impact. That the bear was only slightly older than a cub became irrelevant in time. Future tellings of the tale, by those who were there, rendered the animal as menacing and fierce as a lion, though, in truth, it was only its diminutive stature and light-footed paws which allowed it to get so close in the first place.

It was Aimee's blood curdling scream which first alerted Benjamin to the animal's approach. And, had Jacob Hall not spoken of their threat, Benjamin's response might have been less emphatic. As it was, he emptied the entire magazine of bullets into the meandering mammal, tearing its flesh to shreds and collapsing it to the ground like a fur-clad sandbag.

In the immediate aftermath, Benjamin could barely process the violence. He knew he would never forget the animal's anguished death cry, a wretched mewling plea for salvation which would never arrive. A bloated silence filled the air around them as the light slowly vanished from the creature's eyes.

'Holy shit,' said Tony. 'You killed it, man. You totally killed a bear.'

Benjamin put the gun down on the ground and twisted the barrel towards the river. Glancing around the group, he saw their expressions frozen in a giddy mix of fear and exhilaration. He walked forwards, put a sneaker against the bear's bloodied fur and shoved it into the river with a heavy splash. Part of him expected the animal to rise again from the waters, its eyes lit up with rage as it searched for retribution. Instead, his heart eased its thumping as the animal sank out of sight.

'That was something, man,' said Tony. He took a pack of cigarettes from his pocket and offered one. 'Help yourself, Ben. Can we call you Ben?'

Benjamin nodded. He liked the way his new name sounded, so grown up and concise.

'How about baby killer?' said Rufus.

Ben took one of Tony's cigarettes, took a deep drag then let the smoke trail slowly from his mouth in a gravity-defying waterfall. 'You don't ever speak to me like that again,' he said to Rufus. 'Do you understand me?'

The colour drained from Rufus's face and his eyes became suddenly moist. He had understood very well.

Ben turned around to find Aimee staring at him again, only this time her eyes were filled with sparkle, as if she had stumbled across exactly what she wanted in the last place she thought to look.

'Come on,' she said, offering her outstretched palm to him.

Without another word, they walked hand in hand back towards the woodland path.

***

THE KISS HE would remember forever. Not for its execution, a rather sloppy mess of tongues and teeth which first alarmed then spectacularly thrilled him. Rather that, when he opened his eyes and saw Aimee, she was so gorgeous and radiant that the whole forest seemed to light up around her, a blur of fluorescent greens and perfect beams of sunlight. The moment could not have been more magical.

And then she spoke.

'What was it like?' she said.

'What?'

'To shoot the bear? To kill it?'

Ben had done his best to move on from the incident lest his mind be dragged into despair. 'I didn't feel anything,' he said. 'Not when it happened. I just started shooting.'

'Why?'

'To protect us. To protect you. Because my dad warned me

about bears.'

Aimee shook her head. 'I call bullshit. You must have felt something.'

Ben tried to stifle his irritation. 'I don't want to talk about it.'

'Why?'

'Just because.'

Aimee put her hands on her hips. 'We need to work on this, Ben. The bear, the gun. This makes you a *someone* now. A real person. Don't you see that? You're my boyfriend now. The bear slayer.'

Somewhere in the back of his mind, Ben heard the animal crying out in pain. He shook his head. 'No. I'm not.'

Aimee looked at him blankly. 'What did you say?'

Ben walked forwards, kissed her on the cheek. 'Go back to the others, Aimee.'

'Excuse me –'

'You belong with them. And that's totally fine. No hard feelings, right?'

Aimee's chin began to tremble. 'But I like you,' she said.

Ben scratched at the back of his scalp, bit his lip. There was a few more awkward moments before Aimee's face hardened.

'Asshole,' she said, storming off towards the river.

Ben was alone amongst the towering pines.

***

BY THE TIME he got back to camp, the sun was burning red as it eased towards the horizon line. More fathers had gathered around the roaring campfire, a wax tableau of middle-age waiting to melt beside its flames. No one noticed him standing by the trees. In truth, he did not want to draw near. He had not forgotten that laughter.

It was then he heard his father's voice from near the tents. 'Benjamin?'

Ben stared at him as he approached. 'What?' he said.

'Are you okay?'

'Yeah, Dad. I'm just great.'

Jacob edged closer, reaching his hand towards Ben's shoulder.

'Don't,' said Ben. 'Please. Just leave me alone.' He was fighting back tears now, thinking only of the carcass of the bear, the way its fur had been matted with blood.

'What's wrong?'

Ben shrugged.

'You can tell me.'

Ben thought about Aimee storming off. 'You wouldn't understand.'

Jacob smiled. 'Yeah, I would.'

Ben looked at his father. His eyes were fixed upon him, a keen awareness of a world outside his own concerns. 'Okay,' he said. 'Sure you can handle this?'

'Did they do something to you? The other kids?'

'No. Not at all. They were all cool. Mostly. Rufus was a jackass.'

'His father's a jackass,' said Jacob. 'That's kind of how it goes. What did he do?'

'Nothing really. We were just horsing around. I think I said something that got his back up. And then he said something and I said something else. It was kind of dumb.'

'Are you cool now?'

Ben thought about the look he had seen in Rufus's eyes. 'Absolutely,' he said. 'We're all cool now.'

'What about Aimee?'

Ben felt himself choke up, a sudden sadness washing over him like a riptide over sand. Many things had been lost out in the woods.

Jacob spoke. 'Is that what's got you down, buddy? Aimee?'

Ben shrugged. 'Maybe.'

'I'm sorry, Benjamin. But this stuff happens, man. This feeling, this sadness, it'll pass.'

'How do you know?'

'I just do.'

Benjamin nodded, more for his father's benefit than his own. And then, to his great surprise, Jacob Hall embraced him. 'You got friends, Benjamin. Always remember that. At the very least, you got me,' he said.

Jacob stepped back. There was a glance between them, just long enough for them to see each other as they truly were. And afterwards, they walked side-by-side to the campfire and sat down amongst a sea of smiling grizzled faces.

Cinders After Midnight
Shirley Golden

IT WASN'T LONG before the iron began to frown at her. She tucked it away in the wide, low cupboard beneath the stairs, along with a red bucket that had previously blown raspberries. She hadn't minded that so much—the floors could wait. But there was guilt creased into those stacked linen tablecloths.

Letters tumbled in love as she rearranged words, and tidied sentences so that subjects agreed. She exchanged abstract terms for concrete ones: happily-ever-after became ink.

But the dishcloths began to mutter, so she scrubbed the kitchen sides until bleach infected her senses. Her activities served a dual purpose: surfaces and sponges were appeased.

The files hummed from inside her laptop because they knew she was dying to get back to them. What else was left? Soon her stories would sing.

The vacuum cleaner scowled.

'The floors don't mind,' she snapped.

And in her stubbornness, she ignored calls from the phone.

The printer spat out page after page of crisp, white sheets which contained images of long mahogany hair, tangled in bedside brushes remembered from her youth. It was cathartic, soothing.

But when the ink ran out, she heard the paper snigger—it

had always been an advocate of the wooden floors.

'Don't worry,' she cried and dragged out the old mop that was no longer up to the task, but in the end she made the best of it. It's what she told herself: striving is all. It's the most anyone can do.

EVENTUALLY, HER NEIGHBOURS called social services where they discovered her decomposing body on the hall floor. They made cursory calls and berated the mess. The ink-covered pages they fed into the shredder, without reading a single line.

Her family arrived after the funeral service was complete. They were unable to guess her password, so they flogged her laptop on eBay where a bidding war took place. Who'd have thought anyone would see value in the old thing?

It was posted to a man who lived in St Just. He stumbled upon the correct PIN by virtue of nomenclature: his cat shared its name with the dead woman's passion.

And that was how one night, a man from Cornwall, unlocked her stories. And as he read the screen those words began to sing.

Home Improvements
Joanna Campbell

CLARE ADJUSTED THE position of the bed to allow space for a fair fight. She smoothed the eiderdown and plumped the pillows, ready for Bessie and Marcus to forgive one another later.

She moved the lamp from the lounge to the bedside table, then opened the linen trunk, which was really a matchbox she had wrapped in wood-effect sticky-backed plastic. Inside it she found a crocheted doily, the size of her thumbnail, for the lamp to stand on.

If only Bessie would toss out all these old, mismatched pieces and start again. Far too much sentimental attachment. Although of course Clare understood that change was frightening.

Those tiny tissue-paper flowers, for example. A few years ago, when Clare was six, she had made them for Marcus to give Bessie on the day he proposed. They were faded and worn-out now, but a memory, at least, of better times.

Bessie ought to confront Marcus. Tell him not to cast her aside. Throw the flowers at him if necessary and finish them off with a flourish. She should perch on the edge of the bed to await him, her Victorian petticoats skimming the Turkish rug. No, better move her nearer the door, in case she needed to side-step his temper.

'Oh, you're looking old,' Clare whispered, touching Bessie's startled expression and excessive rouge. 'Your nose is wearing thin and you're almost bald.'

No wonder Marcus had begun shouting at Bessie the minute he came in from work, stomping up the little staircase, his bushy black hair grazing the ceiling.

Clare snapped the end off a matchstick and coloured it with a fleshy felt-pen. She glued it onto Bessie's nose, where it resembled a fungal growth. She snapped a wooden flower off the herbaceous border and pasted it onto Bessie's head to cover her diminishing hair.

Clare bent Bessie's legs into a sitting shape, every joint crackling with the effort. Time had left her tattered and stiff, while Marcus had become more distinguished, although less tolerant, with age.

Marcus was sitting upright on the box of items bought for Clare's last birthday, but not yet unpacked. The box served as his temporary office. He was due to arrive home from work at six. Clare glanced at the clock. Bessie would know her fate in half-an-hour.

Downstairs in the kitchen, Mother was whisking eggs and Father slicing cucumber. A small brick of butter oozed in the pan. It was always omelettes with salad for Friday tea, on the table by a quarter past six. In a few minutes they would call, "Clare! Tea time!" One bass, one soprano. The harmony used to make them laugh.

Father had brought home the weekend gladioli and Mother had bashed the stems, her upper arms slack and quivering these days.

Clare would sit between them at the table and breathe in Father's leathery-office smell and the faint scent of washed lettuce from Mother's hands. Her knuckles were swollen now, securing her wedding ring in position for life.

Home Improvements

On Clare's fifth birthday, the lounge was filled with the biscuity fragrance of *Plum Cottage – Dream Home*, a brand-new wooden dolls' house. Bessie, encased in protective foam-rubber, resembled an Egyptian mummy. Her three-piece-suite and dining table were rolled in corrugated card. Clare arranged them in the house just as they were, and they remained that way until Marcus arrived the following year to offer his hand in marriage.

Downstairs, the two sherry glasses chimed on the silver tray. Clare listened to the quiet conversation, the rising and falling notes of it, the predictable pattern of childhood song: his humid train carriage, her lengthy wait in the greengrocer's queue, the need to cut out the seedy section of the north-facing box-hedge.

Clare knelt on the floor in front of Plum Cottage, straining to decipher individual words.

'Nothing has changed yet,' she whispered.

Last week, when Clare was walking with her class to the swimming-pool, she had seen Father in the shadows of the market square. He was holding hands with his secretary. She was wearing a short, suede skirt, her legs not yet scribbled with inky veins. And last night, Mother was weeping with a wine bottle in the kitchen.

She blotted out these thoughts because it was time for Marcus to come home. This time, before he left the office, he left the lid of the box open.

When he pushed open the front door and stamped inside Plum Cottage, Bessie fell off the bed.

'For heaven's sake, pull yourself together,' Clare said, propping her against the wall. 'Stand up to him, please. We haven't much time.'

But no amount of manipulation could induce Bessie to maintain her poise.

Marcus clattered up the stairs.

'Oh, he's won now,' Clare said. 'You've given up without a fight.'

She pressed her face deep inside Bessie's house so she could support her against the cupboard in the corner. 'Go on. Show him what you're made of.'

Marcus appeared in the bedroom doorway, his papery black suit rustling, his shoulders filling its width and his head brushing the top of the door.

'Get down to the kitchen, you cheating cad!' Bessie shouted, cheeks glowing in the lamplight. 'Go on with you. Last night's supper is still on the table. Don't expect it hot, you rotten good-for-nothing!'

'That's the spirit. Good for you, Bessie,' Clare said.

Mother would be watching the beaten eggs combine in the smoking pan.

'Careful it doesn't catch, dear,' Father would warn as he mandolined the garden beetroot.

Mother was wearing her rose-pink frock today. Pink rejuvenates the complexion, the ladies' magazines advised. Father always removed her apron for her, draping it over the back of her chair before they sat down, the cat pouncing at the dangling ties.

Always the same.

Bessie chased Marcus downstairs. They faced each other in the kitchen. Bessie hurled a plastic lamb chop which hit Marcus full on the nose. She gathered up a sack of potatoes and threw it at him, but he dodged.

The omelette was sizzling.

Pepper grinding.

The telephone rang.

Father took the call in his study, his breath dampening the mouthpiece. Mother scraped her chair away from the table. It creaked as she sank into it.

Marcus kicked the potato sack across the floor. Bessie fell over it. Nothing toppled out because the potatoes were only a piece of printed card stuck into the opening of the sack. Marcus picked up the lamb chop and flung it at Bessie's head. She lay still.

The omelette caught fire.

Out of the open box emerged Stella, new on Clare's last birthday, even though Father deemed her "too old really, for dollies".

Stella still sported the bandeau of soft, clear plastic that kept her hair perfect. Blonde and shop-fresh in her turquoise trouser-suit, she entered the kitchen and linked arms with Marcus.

'If you hadn't let the fight go out of you, Bessie,' Clare said, 'then you'd still have your husband and your lovely home. But you gave in, you clot. You absolute idiot.'

She tucked Bessie away in the box, beneath the tiger-skin rug which Marcus would eventually give as an engagement present to the youthful Stella. Of course, there would have to be a divorce first.

Clare's friend, Annabel, had said her parents squabbled over every stick of furniture. Annabel's mother claimed everything should stay put, so Annabel's life could proceed as if nothing had happened. The father yelled why-the-hell-should-he-leave-with-nothing, then sliced a painting in half with his Stanley knife. The mother took her sewing-scissors to the best table-cloth. Even after all the cheating and fighting and cutting tore them apart, they kept turning back, breathing more fire.

Shortly before her father moved out, Annabel's parents retired to their bedroom and Annabel heard a curious, syncopated panting vibrate through the ventilated heating system. And that was how it should be, Clare reasoned, tasting the salt of a fresh tear in the corner of her mouth. Not sensible conclusions whispered in corners, the division made final with polite smiles and do-have-the-last-slice-of-toast-my-dear-and-how-about-separating?

Clare shredded the tissue-paper flowers to dust.

Annabel was living with her father and his mistress now. The mistress gave Annabel chocolate-mint ice-cream and a pair of patent stilettos for weekends. Not for choir, the father had stipulated, although that didn't stop Annabel slipping them on under her surplice. And because the mistress showed Annabel how to brighten her hair with lemon juice, a boy had asked her for a date. Annabel's friends, mindful of their own tight-lipped mothers with their tight curls, groaned with envy.

Throughout the trauma, Annabel kept up her grades, maintained her four hundred metre hurdles record and, for an extortionate charge, taught a group of fourth-years how to French-kiss. But the heart of Annabel's mother had crumbled like the icing on an ancient wedding-cake, and people said she'd been put away somewhere.

Clare picked up Stella. She was dressed like an air-hostess, impossibly glamorous for the rustic little cottage with its painted wisteria creeping up the walls. She was already turning her nose up at the ill-matched furnishings and home-made extras. She didn't pair at all well with Marcus in his outmoded frock-coat.

Surely he must miss Bessie, faded but familiar, always busy at the stove. If only she could come out again, so her worn wooden hands could wring Stella's neck. But Stella was made of a modern, indestructible vinyl.

Clare coughed from the smoke curling up the stairs. The omelette would have turned to soot by now and, judging by the sudden yelp, Mother must have seared her hand on the hot pan-handle. The voices downstairs had quietened, like the silence before a thunder-clap, and Clare prayed Father was holding his wife's burnt fingers under cold water, dressing the wound with a white bandage.

Clare picked up Plum Cottage and placed it on her bed, this unexpected earthquake muddling its contents. She had done it before, to see how things landed, and to savour the comfort of resettling them.

She peered through a window at the fallen sideboard, the pots and pans jumbled on the kitchen floor, the toppled hat-stand. Bad quarrels between Marcus and Bessie usually lasted at least a full day and night, but this one was different. Clare couldn't leave things alone until tomorrow. It had to be sorted out now, before any more tears came, because it was so hard trying to make them fall in silence.

She opened the entire frontage of the house, detaching it from its hinges and setting it aside so the devastation was clear. It was best to see the whole picture. Before tidying the mess, she tried to make Marcus cling to Stella the way he used to with Bessie. But they wouldn't stay attached. Not only were Stella's limbs too new and inflexible, upon closer inspection it became clear she had not been created with bendable joints.

Clare set them aside and put everything back in place. Then she left her bedroom, went to the landing, climbed onto a chair and pulled the rope that released the loft-hatch. The ladder unfolded. She went up, retrieved the box with *Plum Cottage – Dream Home* printed on it and packed the house inside. At some point during the process, Stella managed to shut herself in the pantry and glue the door shut.

Clare struggled with the box on the ladder, sliding it up one rung at a time, pushing hard until she slotted it home.

Back in her room, she lay down in the growing dark, cupping Marcus and Bessie in her hands. They were at peace with each other now the threat had been removed. Clare apologised for taking their cottage away, but explained they must trust her to sort out something else for them. Not another dream home. It might have to be makeshift at first—a shoe-box perhaps, one with tissue-paper lining—but with the chance of improvements as time went by. As far as she could tell, they appeared to understand.

Impermanent Facts
Lucie McKnight Hardy

SHE'S VACUUMING IN her daughter's bedroom when she remembers that there is a cupboard. In the cupboard there is very little: a few clothes, neatly folded and waiting for the charity shop; a play mat her daughter has no use for now; and a doll's house, devoid of inhabitants.

And then there is the smell.

Acidic, she thinks. Her brain makes an infinitesimal adjustment to the thought. Astringent. Yes, that's more like it. Astringent and green and fresh and sharp enough to summon a memory from her childhood.

The tickle of the ladybirds that alight upon her fingers. Just two at first, their bonfire domes gleam brazen in the sunlight. Then more arrive and settle on her hands. They fold their wings, veil-like, under brittle bonnets. Soon she has a swarm, dozens and hundreds, each one coveting a unique constellation upon its back. They run over her hands and up her arms and onto her face and over her eyelids, and she gives herself up to the prickling, the drumming of tiny feet on her skin as their bodies speckle hers.

She searches her brain for the source of this memory. She plucks at the synapses that bind these thoughts together, the grey matter that acts as glue to unite one evocation with another and suggest a new version of the truth.

She knows there were no ladybirds.

She knows there is no daughter now.

And yet the fragile bodies desiccate and the weight of the vacuum cleaner causes them to crumble and to disappear.

All that remains is the smell.

Roast Potatoes
Rachael Dunlop

AFTER

I WILL PLANT carrots. Parsnips. Turnips. Things that will keep long into the winter. I can't remember the last time I ate a turnip. We used to try to carve them at Halloween. I say 'try' because they were as hard as bullets, bullets the size of babies' heads. Mum wouldn't let me have the sharp knife so I'd spend hours scraping the insides out with a spoon. More often than not the spoon would bend before the turnip would yield. When I was a kid there were no pumpkins in the supermarket, their insides helpfully hollow and scoopable. Imagine: food grown just to play with. Of course, that was before. There are no pumpkins anywhere now.

So I won't plant turnips. Potatoes, though. Definitely potatoes. New potatoes, marble smooth, barely boiled, with pepper and butter, if I can get it. I'll put the larger ones away for mashing and roasting. Roast potatoes, their roughed-up edges butter-crisp, insides like steamed velvet, so hot you have to huff air into your mouth to cool it down before you try to swallow it, but you just couldn't wait and now you're paying the price.

Only there probably won't be enough fuel for roasting potatoes. There's enough to burn the bodies now, but after? What will we burn after?

I won't think about roast potatoes.

I'll take apart the garden shed. Lever nails from wood with a crow bar so the larch-lap panels stay intact. The panels will be good for boarding the windows at the front of the house. Winter is coming.

Winter is always coming. I used to get melancholy in the summer, every day taking me closer to another winter. If I'd known each inexorable turning of season into season was taking me ever closer to now, I'd have savoured more the moments I was living in.

The shed, yes. It'll have to go, so I should make use of it. It will get requisitioned otherwise, some poor soul billeted to sleep there. Tapping on the wired glass of the kitchen door to use my bathroom in the morning. Hoping, vainly, for a hot meal from the oven that'll be no more than a glorified cupboard by then. The gas is so intermittent already, I doubt there'll be any at all soon.

The things we took for granted, ours at the turn of a tap, the flick of a switch. Electricity. Gas. The internet. I never really thought about the people making those things happen. Never considered what it would be like when there weren't enough people. Too many people, that's what we'd worried about. Now there's barely enough.

Selfish of me, I know, not wanting to take in a Wanderer. I have this house, this whole house, and I have you to thank for that. But I'm also a woman on my own, and I have you to blame for that. They'll put a man in the shed, I know they will, and then what?

I won't think about that. Or roast potatoes.

I just need to wait out the winter. Spring will take care of itself.

I'll have to be careful, though, when I dig over the garden, not to disturb the place where we buried the cat. Such a sad time, when everyone's pets were dying and no one knew why and we thought things couldn't get any worse but they did. And now crying for the cat seems like such foolishness even as I pine for her company, the soft sagginess of her belly as it swayed under her legs, the pressing insistence of her jaw jammed into the palm one hand as the other hand found the sweet spot behind her ear.

I won't think about the cat.

I'll have chestnuts for Christmas, foraged from the trees in the park. Eat nuts, they tell us, if you can find them. For the protein. Hazel and cobs and chestnuts. Native nuts. I'll sling a net under one of the trees to catch the chestnuts as they fall, those green spiked bombs with their white flesh and mahogany-red fruits. I saw nets like that skirting the olive trees in Sorrento. I'll never see Italy again. Not unless I walk there.

Damn. I won't have a net. Why would I? What part of my former suburban life would have required a net big enough to sling around a tree? Maybe I could make a net. How do you make a net anyway? If there's any juice left in the generator I will go online and see if any servers are up and I'll do a search. There's bound to be an archived page somewhere that will tell me.

That's all there will be soon. Archive. All that remains of the world I was born into, the world I took for granted, the world that is gone. Images, words, sounds, everything we had and lost. The entire population of the planet a fallen civilisation. Well, that's globalisation for you.

I still sleep on my side of the bed, leaving yours smooth and cool and waiting for you. I didn't see it happen, so there's always a chance it didn't. You weren't anywhere to be seen when it was finally safe for me to venture out of the house. Maybe they took you. Maybe they didn't.

Maybe you died before they even got to you.

I won't think about that. Or the cat. Or roast potatoes.

I'll carry on, though. I'll carry on carrying on because of what you did for me. I'm still breathing because you couldn't.

NOW

THEY'RE COMING. THE rolling rumble of the armoured jeeps is unmistakeable. They are one, maybe two streets away. There is still time. I wish there wasn't.

You're sitting on the floor with your back to the front door, shaking your head at me. 'You have to let me go,' you say. Air sliding so tightly into your squeezed lungs I can barely make out the words. I follow your lips instead. Your lips.

'You can't leave me here alone,' I say, moving towards you. 'We'll be safer together. I can look after you.'

You raise a hand and, weak though you are, I stop. Why do I stop? I should take you by the shoulders, guide you to the hiding place we fashioned when we first heard what was happening. But no, I stop. Because I know you are right. And it is unbearable.

'We'll explain,' I say, 'Tell them it's your asthma. You're not infected. You're not.'

You look up at me as you slide a little further down the door, not wanting to waste energy holding yourself upright. You take a deep breath and the words come clearer. 'Doesn't make any difference. They will take me and then they'll take you. Because of me. I have to go. Now.'

You've been in the process of going for weeks already. Withdrawing, deleting. Piece-by-piece dismantling the evidence of our life together. First to go were the photos, replaced in their frames by generic prints. Then most of your clothes. Your bike. Your laptop, tablet, phone. Books with your name in them. Letters, bills, old cheque book stubs. Contracts cancelled, accounts closed.

Everything you own is now in the bag at your feet. Everything but my heart, which you must leave behind.

I cross the room and sink to the floor at your feet. 'Tell me again,' I say, 'why you have to leave me. Make me believe it.'

'Can't,' you say. 'Too hard. Breathing and talking. You tell me.'

I speak slowly, matching the rhythm of your shallow breaths, the short rise and fall of your upper chest. 'They are taking people who are infected. With this disease. And people they think are infected. With this disease. Except we don't even know if it is a disease. Maybe it's something in the water. Or the air.'

You fidget, shift against the door. I know that gesture of old, your impatience with my tendency to go off on tangents.

'Okay, okay,' I say. 'They are taking everyone they think may have this breathing disease, and they take the people who live with them too, even if they show no symptoms. We don't know where they are taking them, but we know no one has ever come back, sick or not. Yes?'

You nod.

'And whether or not you have this disease or it's just your asthma, they're coming for you because you are sick.'

You nod again.

'If you leave now, I'll be safe.'

Nod.

'I'll tell them you moved out months ago. And then I'll be safe.'

Nod.

'I'll be safe and you'll be dead.'

A pause, I hear you gathering your breath as deep as you can into your lungs. You have something to say. 'I'll be dead either way. No more inhalers. Nebulisers. Steroids.'

You're right, of course. When the antibiotics stopped working, the fragility of human existence was exposed, raw to see. Sometimes I think antibiotics were the worst thing that happened to human beings. The further we removed ourselves from death, the more arrogant we became. Incaution no longer had consequences. And now other medicines are running out too. In previous generations you and your asthma wouldn't have survived beyond childhood. For the generations that come after us (should there be any), it will be the same. It felt like progress, our mastery of disease. But it has been our undoing. We never had it so good. And none will ever have it as good again.

So there you sit, propped against our front door, a man who should never have grown to manhood. The jeeps have stopped moving, their engines idling. I strain for the sound of metal doors creaking, slamming, the pliant sound of rubber-soled boots hitting tarmac. I go to the bay window and press my cheek to the glass.

'Can't see them yet,' I say. 'Maybe they've gone the other way.'

You drag yourself up, grab your bag, you're out the door before I can stop you. I see now what you've been saving your energy for. You turn away from the sound of the soldiers, putting as much distance between yourself and our home as you can. There is shouting, running, and I turn away from the window. I can't look. In the fireplace, the burned remains of your driver's licence, passport, library card. You are out there now, a man with no name, no past, no future. Saving mine.

I go upstairs and slide into your side of the bed. There is more give in the mattress here from the weight of you, night after night, year after year. There's a crack in the ceiling, running from edge to edge, bisecting the circle of the light fitting. It looks just the same from your side and mine. I shuffle myself over to the other side of the bed, pull the duvet under my chin and close my

Roast Potatoes

eyes. When I was a tiny child, waiting for Father Christmas to come, I'd keep my eyes tight shut, as instructed. But every now and then, between fitful sleepings, I would scoot down to the bottom of the bed and wriggle my toes, to see if he'd been yet, if he'd weighted the stocking I had left with tangerines and walnuts, sugared jellies and chocolate coins, pens and puzzles, plastic gems and bouncy rubber balls.

Now I imagine the length of the cat stretched out at the foot of the bed, her belly just a toe-poke away and you asleep behind me, filling the space you left in your shape. I search the archive of my memories, slide back in time, make the weight of you behind me real, and think about roast potatoes.

BEFORE

'I THINK YOU love that cat more than you love me,' you said.

It was a Sunday. A lazy, lovely half-dozing morning cast in soft shadows by an early-Spring sun, the duvet softened to the shape of us, the cat trying to find a place to mould to her own heft.

'The cat was here before you,' I said. This conversation, or variants on it, is one we'd had many times before. Teasing transformed into incantation, the back and forth that bound us together. 'If your asthma gets really bad, I mean life-threateningly bad, I'll reconsider the pecking order.'

You didn't reply, but rolled away from me, your curled back an invitation. I rolled over too, cupping myself into you, my nose poked into the soft place between your shoulder blades.

You wriggled. 'Geroff, that tickles,' you laughed. I loved to make you laugh.

I let my eyes focus on your shoulder. A permanent indentation there from the weight of your shoulder bag. All the things you took to work every day: laptop, tablet, chargers, free papers picked up at the Tube station but never read. A bottle of water, the plastic thin and crinkly, doing their bit for the environment they said, reducing the packaging. I said you should just fill a bottle from the tap. And you agreed, but somehow always forgot.

I ran a finger along that indentation. A beast of burden.

'Why do you have so many things?' I asked. 'Do you really need to take them all to Canary Wharf every day?'

You sighed and I heard it then, the catch in your chest. You coughed to cover it up. I slid my hand from your shoulder to the flat of your back, my palm against your ribs, as if I could send the heat from my heart to your lungs, ease them into relaxing. Easy. Easy.

'I'll be first against the wall come the revolution,' you said, 'just for being so bloody useless. Breathing is a pretty basic function. It would be nice to at least get that right.'

'Sweetheart,' I said, and you rolled back towards me, slowly so I had time to duck under your arm and lay my head on your chest. The cat shifted and a daze of dander rose in the warming air. We both watched it in silence.

'I'll find someone to take the cat,' I said at last, 'just until you're better.'

You wriggled your toes under the cat's belly and she sprang up, pouncing on the monster that had suddenly appeared under the duvet. 'Let's not think about that now,' you said.

'What's for lunch?' I asked.

'Roast chicken.'

'And?'

'Carrots. Roasted with red onions and garlic.'

My mouth was beginning to water, my fingers travelling the line of dark hair that ran from your chest bone to navel.

'And?'

Roast Potatoes

'Mmm,' you said, finding it hard to focus. 'Potatoes.'

'What sort of potatoes?'

'Mashed?'

I pinched a hair between two fingers and tugged.

'Ouch!' you said. 'Okay, not mashed. Roast. Roast potatoes.'

'Better than the ones my mother used to make?'

'Never,' you said, 'Nothing can be better than the memory of perfection.'

And you were right. Nothing could be better.

The Distance
Keren Heenan

TOO SOON SHE is there. The corner turned, the old cypress in view, and she's slowing down for the bridge. Even before she gets there she can hear the familiar rumble and clatter, *ba-bob ba-bob*, of tyres over the wooden planks. And then the tyres hit and there it is – *ba-bob ba-bob*, bringing a wave of memories she'd thought long gone. Returning from outings late at night, she asleep, or at least pretending to be, in the back seat watching the pin-prick of stars framed by the window – wondering about the sound they make when they first come out; a crinkling sound she always thought, like crumpling cellophane. The dark, a warm blanket. The motor droning and tyres humming on the bitumen. Heave of the motor slowing, then *ba-bob ba-bob*, and she'd know she only had to keep her eyes closed, go floppy and her father would lift her up like a baby and carry her to her bed. 'Let her walk, Dan, she's not a baby,' her mother would say, and he'd silence her with a perfectly weighted *shhh*.

The oily scent of his hair hits her for a moment, then it is gone, and she's skidding on the gravel, climbing the steep driveway. When she reaches the top she sees that her mother has been keeping a look out. She's standing near the porch, one hand shading her eyes, then she waves, a quick jerky movement of her hand, as if she's not sure she knows the driver. Or perhaps it's a fly she's brushing away. Esther returns the wave and her mother waves again, this time with confidence, a certain verve to her movements, as if Esther is royalty and her car is but passing by.

When she pulls up, Esther leans down for her bag. Her head out of view, she makes the most of this brief time; grimaces, breathes in slow and long then lifts her head. Her mother is at the passenger side window, watching her. She wears a green wrinkled cardigan and a wan smile and holds her head to one side. She mouths something through the window that Esther thinks may be, 'there you are,' and Esther knows the time has come to get out of the car. Be a daughter to this person she barely recognises. She opens the door and the breeze hits her in the face, a 'stiff' breeze, her father would have said. She'd never thought to ask, why *stiff*, how can a breeze be stiff? But she thinks it now as she pulls her collar up, hunching her shoulders.

'Esther, dear,' her mother has her arms open, waiting for her. Esther lifts her handbag onto her shoulder and walks into the embrace, leaning forward from the waist. Beneath her hands and arms her mother's frame feels diminished; she is thin and rigid. Esther feels her own rigidity and thinks of two planks of wood placed apart, leaning towards each other, the smallest of touches.

She pulls away but leaves one hand lightly on her mother's arm. 'I'm sorry it's been so long,' she says. 'It's just such a long flight. London's a world away,' then she stops. Excuses. She wasn't going to offer excuses.

They turn to go inside, her mother steering her away from the side door. 'It doesn't open. There's ... things in the way.' Esther thinks, boxes; she's already started the packing process, and she's pleased that it won't be left to her to crack the whip. The back door only opens halfway and they both have to turn sideways to get through the door.

'What's with the door?' Esther shoves at the door and closes it behind them. She sees then what has caused the problem; boxes and bags stacked almost to the ceiling. 'Wow, you have been busy. Clearing out stuff already.'

Her mother stands in front of her, mouth opening and closing, sucking her lips as if she's about to speak then stops. Finally she says; 'Well, not really. It's … it's things I want … I want to keep.'

'Right. Well, they better be important things. Remember, there won't be much room there. I think they said one small wardrobe, a couple of drawers and a shelf. So you really do have to, you know, cull a lot of—' She sees her mother's face, and once again the word *diminished* comes to mind. Her mother is not the tyrant she remembers. She is small, broken almost, and her eyes, even paler, as if the blue has leached away over time. There is still the darker flare around her pupils that Esther thinks an iridologist may diagnose as digestive problems.

But before, back when she'd be hunched and trembling in front of her mother, having done something 'unforgiveable' – broken a cup, lost a book, fell in the mud – back then, the darker flare seemed to pulsate in those pale blue eyes and there seemed something unhinged, something inestimable about her, and Esther's speechless rigidity would only inflame the situation. If her father was there he'd rescue Esther with quietly spoken words, 'Leave her, Mary.' Now, when Esther looks into her eyes, there is none of that icy-blue glare of impatience, no steel. Now, those same eyes hold a plea, and it's not until she enters the kitchen that Esther knows the nature of that plea.

She stands in the doorway, turning her head from the table to the stacked benches covered in an assortment of things tumbled across the surface: figurines, salt and pepper shakers, a meat grinder, pencils, chipped cups, alarm clock, a shoe, measuring tape, iron, a pile of clothing, and other things she can't identify.

A small cleared space at one end of the table is occupied by a cup, a plate and a teapot. But the rest of the table groans under the weight of boxes, bags, papers and bottles. A chipped mixing bowl overflows with cardboard tubes, scrunched plastic wrap, shoelaces, screws, string, a waffle iron, envelopes. Her mother had always been a collector of all things Royal – births, deaths and marriage paraphernalia – of teaspoons, of postcards sent by travellers. But the current stacks of items are not so much collections as random items with no apparent rationale, no common theme.

'Mu-um ...' Esther starts, but she doesn't know what comes next.

Her mother pushes past her and stands against the table, hands splayed defensively. 'I'll ... I'll sort through it,' she says. 'I'm just getting started.'

'Mu-um ...' Esther tries again, quieter, almost a whisper. She takes her handbag from her shoulder and looks around for somewhere to put it. Thinks she may never find it again in all this chaos and returns to the back door to hang it on the handle. She pushes her sleeves up, breathes deep. 'Mum,' she surveys the kitchen again, and when she thinks of what the rest of the house may hold, she is engulfed by an overwhelming sense of futility. What can one piece of plastic wrap in a bin – she looks around, *what bin! Where is a bin*? – what can that mean for the overall scene here? She is not going to look at the rest of the house, not yet. Not until the table is cleared. 'Mum, we're going to have a cup of tea. We'll start here,' she lifts the bowl to the small cleared space. Her mother's eyes follow the trajectory of the bowl, the crease between her eyebrows intensifying but she doesn't speak.

Esther moves the teapot, cup and plate to the already crowded sink. 'A bag, Mum, where's a bag, lots of them?' Her mother turns one way then the other, but she's not really looking, Esther sees, she's just turning around. Esther opens a plastic bag on the table. Newspapers. Most look to be unread, still crisply uncreased, the date recent. 'Why do you …? Do you read these? You should just cancel the subscription if …'

'Your father liked the papers. Every morning over breakfast. I couldn't … I just thought, I might read them, one day, do the crossword. Your father'd always call out the clues to me, don't know why, he always knew the answers.'

'But, Mum, seven years! He's been gone seven years now!' She is almost shouting, and then they look at each other without speaking. In the silence she hears something slide to the floor from the end of the table, and their eyes follow the sound to a pamphlet advertising solar panels. Esther breathes in deep, then out in a rush through her mouth. 'I'm taking these to the recycling bin,' she says lifting the bag. 'Then at least we'll have a bag.'

'But … Lil,' her mother points vaguely in the direction of the closest house; 'She could use them for Kitty Litter,' she takes a step forward, her hand out.

'Lil can get her own Kitty Litter,' Esther says through clamped teeth. 'Besides, there's plenty more. When's bin day?'

Her mother shakes her head. 'I don't know, dear.'

'I'll find out from the Council.'

The recycling bin has a mesh of densely packed cobwebs around the lid. The webs stretch, sticky and elastic, then tear with a soft brushing sound. Inside, the bin is almost empty, apart from some old newspapers and a couple of plastic bottles. A redback spider waves a leg at her from under the lip of the lid and she drops the lid backwards and open, tips in the papers and shakes the bag out. 'Step one,' she mutters. She checks the rubbish bin. It too is almost empty.

Back inside, her mother hasn't moved, though the pamphlet has been placed carefully on top of the boxes. She turns her pale eyes to Esther and says, 'Did you find the bins?' Esther nods. 'I haven't been able to find them,' she says, her palms out, as if that is an excuse, the reason for all of this.

Esther shakes her head. 'They're just out by the garden shed. Same place.'

'Oh-h,' she nods, her hand rubbing idly at her cheek.

Esther takes the plastic wrap and cardboard tubes from the bowl and drops them in the rubbish bag.

'They could be handy,' her mother's voice is tentative, her hand out, ready to retrieve anything should Esther cave in. But Esther doesn't even look her way, she is focused on emptying at least one receptacle. Wants to be able to turn to her and say: 'This is how it will be done.'

Her mother stands watching, pressing her hands, first one then the other, her eyes locked on each item as it is pitched into the bag. It is only when Esther comes to the string that she moves forward, her fingers splayed. 'Now that could be useful, dear. It just needs unravelling.' And Esther hands her the tangle of string and continues with her task. When she empties the bowl she looks over at her mother, her hands, veined and knobbled with arthritis, picking at knots, straightening and winding the string. She doesn't look up when Esther passes her with more papers for the bin. When she returns, she's holding the ball of string in one hand, the other hand stroking it as if it were a small bird.

'Put it with the jaffle-iron,' Esther says. 'That can be the *to-be-sold* pile.'

'Sold? But I could use it.'

'Oh, what for, Mum?'

'It's not a matter of ... of what for. It's just, I could use it, I might want it.'

Esther shakes her head. 'No, it goes into this pile,' and she takes the small bird of string from her mother's hands and dumps it beside the jaffle-iron. 'Three piles, right? This one, *To Sell*, we'll have a garage sale. This one, *Rubbish*,' and she points and moves around as she speaks. 'This one,' she hesitates, she doesn't want to give her the option, 'the *Maybe* pile, maybe sell, maybe throw. Then anything that doesn't sell goes to charity.' Her mother nods, following Esther's pointing finger as if the piles are already there, abandoned, begging to be saved.

Esther works her way across the table and then to the bench, flinging, or placing breakables, to one of the three corners. Her mother shuffles between the piles, sometimes taking from the *Rubbish* pile and placing in the *Maybe* pile. It had taken some time for her to realise there was no *To Keep* pile. That the best she could try for was the *Maybe* pile. When she asked Esther about this, Esther just shook her head. 'You won't need kitchen stuff, Mum. All your meals will be done for you.'

'But I like cooking.'

'I know, but you don't need to anymore,' and she looked away so she didn't have to see her mother's face.

Now with the table cleared and some bench space, she sits her down and puts on the kettle. Leans against the bench and watches her mother's hands sweep across the expanse of table in front of her. 'Mum,' she waits for her to turn. 'How often do you have visitors?'

'Visitors? I don't have visitors, dear.' She turns back to the table, sweeping the laminex tabletop with her hands, as if there is something she must remove from the surface.

'What about Uncle Thomas? What about Lil and Doug, or …' but she can't think of anyone else, apart from herself, who may visit. 'Uncle Thomas said he's been here.' But why didn't he mention the mess, the hoarding of junk, her rumpled appearance? Just a cursive note: *You'll need to come home and help organise your mother; the house is too big for her now, she needs to move into a*

Home. These are the arrangements. Then a list of phone numbers and contacts: Estate agent, Solicitors, Bank, Retirement Home.

'Thomas, oh no, I didn't let him come in. I hadn't cleaned up. He'd just go away thinking what a … what a mess the place was in. No, no, I … I just said I was … in a rush, something like that.'

In the seven years since her father's death, no one has visited, or rarely anyway; no neighbours, no friends, no family members. Thomas being the only other direct family member, apart from Esther herself.

She looks at the back of her mother's head, the swirl of hair at the crown, her pink scalp. A tag hangs out the back of her crushed cardigan. Esther feels something cold lurch around in her chest. So easy, thousands of kilometres away to think that the occasional letter or phone call would be enough. That everything would just take care of itself. She flinches at the memory of her annoyance at Thomas' letter: the *couldn't you do it* thoughts, the *I'm too busy to drop everything* plea. Relief that she hadn't actually responded that way. Rather, she'd groaned and sighed inwardly but applied for leave, finalised Thomas' arrangements, martyr-like. Booked the ticket. Thinking that after it's all over she can return to London to look for somewhere more permanent, with her mother being seen to, the house sold; should give her a chance to put a deposit on something nice for herself. Perhaps somewhere outside London, one of those quaint little villages, duck pond and a cottage garden perhaps.

She wraps her arms around herself, hugging her elbows, and stares at her mother's rounded shoulders. She leans over and tucks in the tag. Her mother looks up, surprised, and catches Esther's hand, holds it for a moment on her shoulder. 'So good to see you, dear. I'm sorry about … all this. It just… got away from me.'

Esther nods. 'I know.' She makes the tea, locates two clean

cups and they sit quietly, listening to the clock, gulp of the fridge, the dirge of a crow somewhere close outside.

Her mother looks up suddenly, turns her head from one side of the kitchen to the other. 'Where's all my newspapers gone?'

A quiet dread creeps over Esther. 'Newspapers? I … took them to the bin, remember?'

'Oh-h. So you did,' she nods, 'So you did,' quietly.

Esther watches her mother's face; her eyes are blinking rapidly, her head sinking slowly to her chest. 'Mum, do you think … have you been forgetting some things lately? More than, say, before?'

'I don't know, dear. Maybe I have.' She looks up at Esther; 'I remembered you were coming,' turns her head away. 'But there's not much else to remember, is there? I just get up, potter about, watch some TV, go to bed.'

'What about the bills, Mum? Are they all paid on time?'

'Oh-h,' she sits up straight, turns her head to one side as if trying to listen for a distant sound. 'No, I don't know anything about bi-ills,' she drags the word out into two syllables. And that cold wave of dread steals over Esther again. 'Thomas has arranged all that.'

Esther realises she's been holding her breath, and she breathes out, audibly. 'Right. Okay. Well … that's good then, easier for you.' And she thinks again of her uncle's brief note. Now, rather than *I'm just too busy*, she hears an order, a smarting reprimand, *Come and see for yourself…* and she swallows, reaches out and places her hand over her mother's at the table edge.

If they could just stay like this, Esther thinks, her hand over her mother's, both of them staring at the same spot on the now cleared table, she could re-imagine another childhood for herself. One where friends were welcomed, could run and jump and scream and turn couches and blankets into cubbies the way she'd done at her friends' houses. Where dogs, rabbits or cats were brought inside and dressed up in doll's hats and baby clothes and offered cups of tea. And skinned knees and ripped dresses were worthy of sympathy, a lolly even. Then, she may have come back home often enough to form an adult relationship with her mother. But she'd only ever returned for her father, a relationship where no effort was required. When he died it no longer mattered to her how far away she moved. And London seemed just the right distance away.

Esther removes her hand, pushes back the chair. 'Just going to take a look around,' she says.

Her mother looks up, alarmed at first, then nods. 'Your old room,' she says, and Esther pauses, imagines the same cluttered state as the kitchen, wonders how that will feel. The last time she'd stayed, for her father's funeral, the room had already been in disarray; part office, part store room, part sewing room. She walks out into the passageway. She doesn't look into the lounge-room, her mother's room, the bathroom. She continues on to the room at the end of the passage, turns the knob and walks in.

She stands still, staring ahead, her mouth open. One hand trails from the door knob down to her thigh. It is as if she has just come in after school. Everything from her pre-high school days has been reinstated; the flowery curtains, the stuffed blue dog on the pillow, quilted bedspread, the cream carpet. Everything in its place. Even the small wooden owl and glass fairies have been returned to the window sill from the cupboard where she'd tossed them, attempting to redo her room into some sort of teenage style – posters and no fiddly toys. She turns around.

Hanging from the wardrobe door is a dress. Not just any dress, but one that brings clear and sharp memories crashing in: the fence, the terrible tearing sound, the dread, the sticky tape, and the rage. She walks over to the dress and holds the fabric in her hand, turning the hem around and around trying to find the tear, the yellowed tape.

Behind her the door opens with a slow whisper over the carpet. She turns as her mother says, 'I stitched it up for you,' as if it were just yesterday Esther had miscalculated the climb over the picket fence, forgetting she was wearing a dress that billowed out behind her. 'There's not much sticky tape is good for. Paper, that's about all.' And she smiles that small pale smile again. 'It was a nice dress. A new one,' she adds, and Esther knows that they both see memories of their own.

Maybe she won't notice – the memory slides in in all its naive stupidity. Of course she noticed the sticky tape pulling the edges of the rip together. Her mother's eyes had flared and she rampaged around vowing, 'Never again, no more new clothes,' until Esther's father stepped in the door – 'Leave her, Mary.'

Esther lays the dress over her arm, holding it by the hanger. It is smaller than she remembers, the collar blue when she'd thought it to be white. When she locates the ridge of stitching just above the hem, she sees a faint yellowing where the tape has stained the white fabric. She looks up and into her mother's eyes; she is close enough to see the blue flare tremble. Esther knows there are old words that could wound.

Leave her, Esther; it is as if her father is there at her shoulder.

'I stitched it up for you,' her mother repeats. 'When I knew you were coming.'

The Land of Bondage
Bettina Daniel

LET US GO then, you and I, to the grocery store, and then separately to the cleaners and the drugstore, where you will make the calls that you say are about work but I suspect are to the colleague you are sleeping with. We will meet as usual on the sidewalk in front of Starbucks. I will round the corner and wave gaily at you with one arm, the other clutching my DVF dresses and your striped shirts. You will wave back and hang up, and in that moment of hello and goodbye I try to read whether the expression on your face is meant for her or for me. We will settle into the car and make our plan for the afternoon, which might be the garden, where we will work side-by-side in our own little worlds. Or might be "golf" for you (we know what that means) and "girl stuff" for me, which is shopping, or a massage, or an appointment with my trainer, the point being indulgence, because it's been a hard week and I deserve it.

This has been going on for some time. I suppose it has reached some kind of stasis. She doesn't want to leave her little girls and earnest husband, and you don't want to incur the upheaval and expense of a divorce. We are, after all, used to each other, companionable, and have long ago codified our domestic expectations to mutual satisfaction. We like our house, which sucks up both of our large incomes. The effort we put into our prestigious jobs is grueling. We're not getting any younger.

A lot of people like us split when the kids go to college, telling themselves the kids wouldn't mind so much then, as if their need for a home transfers to their freshman dorm room. Hah. And we wonder why kids binge drink.

So every Saturday I wonder if you will choose golf. I think about the effort she has to make to tart herself up, make excuses to her husband, and find the frantic energy to tear your clothes off in some convenient hotel room. You are wearing a golf shirt so there's no biting off of buttons, and you're a little thick around the middle these days, but she doesn't have much imagination so would need to do it the way she sees in movies. All that energy. As opposed to the friendly nudge of the foot you used to give me back when we made love, in bed, reading the *New Yorker* or the *Atlantic*. I'd reach for the light switch while finishing a paragraph, saying something smartassy and tossing my white linen nightshirt across the room with a flourish.

Saturday mornings are also the time we talk about the kids, when we need to "talk about the kids," their issues moving like an unpredictable piece of music, Slater's anorexia rising and falling in long, slow arcs in the upper registers while Boyle's asthma and depression beat an irregular bass rhythm. At one point his depression had taken center stage, but abated with a change of major and medication, just as Slater's eating disorder blossomed into a full-throated screech of crisis. This required a week off of work by me and a large bite of our almost-paid-off home equity loan to pay for eating disorder treatment at a luxurious former hunting lodge on the Eastern Shore of Maryland. It was so remote that the electrified perimeter was almost completely buried by dense wetland, except at the unmarked front entrance, where there is no sign or name, but a small red notice that says "danger" in three languages. Otherwise you might think you were approaching Mandalay. That program might have worked by itself; we'll never know. Just then a competing crisis of sexual identity triggered by a foodie with large sleepy eyes and thick black hair took her eye off the ball of methodically starving herself to death. Eventually she got back to college – the highly selective institution that regarded job preparation as beneath their notice, and where we were made to feel lucky to be paying full tuition. As far as we can tell, she's back to boys, and her liking girls seems to be a phase I've been informed is known as lesbian until graduation (or "LUG," if this sort of thing is part of your everyday conversation). Phase or not, it is a huge relief to have her back in the land of normal eaters, or even binge dieters, rather than self-starvers. Sometimes I find myself wanting to send the thick-haired foodie a thank-you note.

Slater's graduation festivities, seemingly designed to search and destroy whatever holdouts of cash that had survived the seven-year assault of tuition and rehab, celebrated each student's staggering brilliance and individuality. It was followed by a trip to a newly chic Caribbean island, together with friends whose prodigious consumption of controlled substance in their early years together had likewise produced expensive detours on the path to graduation. A week of sustainable, eco-friendly indulgence, body scrubs, meditation and bespoke cocktails would ease their transitions to esoteric graduate programs, unpaid venture capital internships in soon-to-emerge markets, or Teach for America placements in cities prominent in the narrative of American decline.

Slater, improbably absorbed by her work in remedial early childhood education, has become a less dramatic topic of our conversation. Her demands for cash – in the form of curt texts – are unencumbered by affection. She has made it clear that our professions – corporate lawyer and industry lobbyist – are dedicated to advancing income inequality, which she sees daily in the erratic earning patterns of her students' adult caregivers. These texts are humbling moments that you and I endure together, locking eyes after reading aloud, and smiling with a relieved, sad shake of the head. She might be obnoxious and entitled, maybe a little cruel – but she is alive and employed.

For the moment it is Boyle who absorbs our allotment of parental attention with his frequent, needy bleats. We respond to his texts deliberately, balancing unconditional love and the suggestion of resources as finely as we can, feeling like elephants trying not to trample the flowers. Then days go by where we wonder if he has gotten through his bad patch, or "lost his battle with depression" as the euphemism goes. Through trial and error we have learned that he answers about one in ten phone calls, which we each make while waiting in traffic or standing in line at Whole Foods, and flaunt our successes at each other like little boys catching fish too small to eat.

But today was not to be a day for Boyle phone calls or the garden, or even golf. Today you say you have an errand to run at Tysons Galleria. This is a destination too gaudily horrendous to be made up, leaving me puzzled – but not for long, because my toes need doing, and the prospect of reading mind-numbing fashion magazines beckons.

SATURDAY NIGHT IS traditionally date night. Sometimes we go to the club and sometimes we stay home and I cook something and set the table and you open a good bottle of wine and we try to look nice. These are meant to be relaxing, which means we don't stay home when there's something risky to discuss.

'Why don't we go to the club tonight?' you say.

I try to look nonplussed. 'Sure.'

The club is an enclave of green surrounding a gracious stone mansion that has gone from Revolutionary era private home to 19th century hunt club to 20th century business expense to 21st century bragging rights for the one percent. We spent years eating at the "new building" – the cavernous barn of a place the club built for members who can't force their children into anything north of a hoodie. These days we are back in the dining room at the main clubhouse, a safe house for those who sniffily enforce standards against barbarian invasion. This change of venue is an immense relief – having launched, more or less, our own offspring we've no desire to watch others go through the same unsightly process.

The old dining room, a short walk away, is another world altogether. There, amid the high ceilings and traditional furnishings and rather nice paintings – all virtually unchanged since my own years as a bratty teen – we feel like visitors to a foreign country last visited under the old regime. The fact that everyone in the dining room is doddering around in bouffant hair and hearing aids makes us feel giddily young.

'I've been thinking,' you say after the octogenarian hostess seats us and shuffles off.

My stomach flutters.

'Maybe we should do something different.'

I see, in slow motion, the celestial axe fall. This will be the end of the years of putting up with and settling for and trying really hard (within reason) – the baby pictures and the wedding pictures and the vacation pictures – the curtains and the silver and the buttons and the bread. Someone in the distance is pouring gasoline from a rusted red can all over everything. Red clouds speed by. Horse hooves clatter. Helicopter blades whir. Big reaping machines with wheels of long, sharp prongs sputter to life.

The waiter wants to tell us about the wines. You listen with patience and order a bottle of our usual. The waiter brings this with the stately sluggishness that is the club's hallmark, giving me time to make a mental list of friends to consult and lawyers to call. Caroline had a good divorce lawyer – a real pit bull – but that left her husband so shattered the children never forgave her. The children – our children – what would they think? My mother, with her mildly disapproving sympathy? The firm? They just named me a senior partner with the emphatic expectation of business development; everyone knows a divorce takes you off your stride.

In fact, I *had* considered the possibility of divorce. I had cast it in the light of a freer life – more vacations, girls' nights out, spa trips, spreading out over the whole house. No excuses. Indulging my interests without apology. Maybe taking up a painting class to fill the hours a husband used to fill. But even while fantasizing, I knew divorce would spell loss. No one to chatter to with bedhead, in jammies. No one to help with the house, pick up restaurant checks, carry luggage, dance with at weddings.

I looked back at you, nodding approval at the waiter and watching him pour as if it took two of you, concentrating, to keep any drops of red off the white tablecloth. The bottle slowly comes up, and bows to my glass. In the silence, three large drops fall and spread slowly through the starched linen fibers.

'Different?' That seemed an unduly euphemistic word for the emotional carnage you have in mind. You will have to do better than that.

You sip and lean back.

'I've been thinking about doing something different this year. Now don't jump to conclusions' – a smile here, as if we're talking about different people altogether – 'because I know this isn't what you were planning on.'

The Land of Bondage

I put on the most opaque face I can. I'm not going to make this easy.

'I've been doing some thinking, and I feel like we've grown apart.' You pause to see how I'm taking it. Stonily, is how.

'And I know you enjoy the comforts.'

So, you've been consulting a lawyer too.

'But maybe this year we should go on a trip that – well, that exercises us differently.'

What on earth are you talking about?

'So I was thinking about the Camino.'

I must have my mouth open, because you tell me so, and then resume.

'You've heard of the Camino? In Spain?'

I feel like we're having two different conversations. 'You mean the walk from France to the cathedral in Santiago?'

You nod, glad that it registers.

My hair, which has been standing on end, starts to relax. An article from *Travel & Leisure* comes into focus. Lots of green and people in hiking boots. 'Oh, yes,' I manage, trying to find my footing.

You lean forward. 'It's like a long hike. The whole thing takes 45 days, but' – you put up your hands at my budding objection – 'but you can make it as short or as long as you like. You can walk six miles a day or twelve miles a day. You can bike it, or even ride a horse.'

I contemplate the idea of riding again, seeing the world from an equine height, hair streaming, except you have to wear a helmet now. I always looked good leaping off a horse, with my long legs – I suppose with practice I could still manage that but I'd have helmet head. This distracts me.

Then I start to get it. 'So was that your errand today?' I ask, eyebrow cocked.

You smile sheepishly. 'I was at L.L. Bean, checking out their quick-dry pants. And underwear. Not that we'd be carrying everything on our back' – no, I think, that's for sure – 'but we'd only have one night in each place. So you need things that dry fast.'

Big thoughts are distracting me, and you mistake that for distaste at a non-luxury vacation. You begin to talk fast.

'It's not like we have to stay at hostels. I mean, of course not. There are some really nice hotels most places. And depending on the route we take – there are lots of different ones – we can find the ones we like best. Pools, if we want. And it's good exercise…'

On you go. The trails through woods and the occasional town. The little churches. The companionship. The simplicity. The reflection. The yellow arrows. The scallop shell and its meaning. The history.

Tonight I will go online, not to look up divorce lawyers, but the Camino. The Camino of Santiago de Compostela. I suppose I'll find tour packages, and blogs full of advice, and pictures of beatific faces. The magazine had shown twee, spontaneous shrines made of rocks and flowers – walking sticks of gnarled wood – and café bars in the middle of the woods.

I consult my iPhone and find, on an Irish site, a page on "Upmarket Lodgings" that sounds promising. Until I realize that "upmarket" means a hotel room with a bathroom. More digging around and I see that one bag is the limit. And not a big one, either. What would I wear to dinner? The pictures showed people eating dinner in their hiking clothes. Did they even get to shower first?

'You really want to do all this walking?' I ask, skeptically.

'Yes,' you say, with more enthusiasm than I expect. 'And no laptop! There's not a lot of connection, anyway.'

No laptop. No connection. I couldn't remember the last time

when I had spent more than the span of a meal – with you or anybody else – without a screen to shield me.

'So… are you game?'

I gulp and fake my best look of confidence. I think about packing only simple clothes. Leaving the computer behind. Checking out of everything for ten days and walking through rainy forests with you, this man I thought I knew everything about, but now seems not to be having an affair. I wonder what else I've been missing.

The butterflies fluttering in my stomach have become large flying dinosaurs. I put on my cockiest face. 'Sure!' I say.

The Martha Rhymes
Susan Breall

AS A CHILD I would always pay my final respects to members of our town who passed away by attending their estate sales. I'd say a silent little prayer for the dead as Bun and I went rummaging through their personal belongings. Bun was my pet rabbit, and although her true name was Flori Bundas she would answer to the name of Bun and come running to me whenever I called her. She was smart enough to stay right by my side during these estate sale outings and never run off, helping me paw through various items of interest at each sale.

    These sales were hosted in the front yards of surviving family members in the heat of August. The sales always happened in late summer, never spring or fall. It didn't much matter when the neighbor died or how important or well-liked the neighbor was in our town. Their sons and daughters, grandsons and granddaughters would wait until the end of the summer to sell off the last worldly possessions of the departed. Young children set up lemonade stands on the dirt roads in front of the houses while the rest of the town strolled leisurely by in the heat, rifling through all the discarded belongings of the deceased, neatly piled on top of card tables or the front lawns. This had been a time-honored tradition for decades in our town of Glen Ellen.

    Sometimes I used to think that some of the very old men and

women I saw rummaging through estate sale items looked like rummage themselves. Bun and I used to sit impatiently at our own lemonade stand watching them. Once in a while I would shout out and beckon them over to our table to sample my special home-made pink lemonade mix so they could quench their parched throats.

One very dry August day in the late afternoon when I was eleven-years old I remember being particularly restless as I sat and sold lemonade at my usual spot under a tall walnut tree. Business had been slow, so I decided to pocket my earnings, grab Bun under my arm, and walk through all the front yards of the neighbors who happened to be hosting estate sales that year. I hoped to round up some neighborhood kids to play kick ball. I also went to see if there were any special estate sale items I could afford to buy. School was starting up again soon and my mother told me to look for a good winter coat and a nice pair of gloves.

We headed purposefully towards the dead-end part of the street where Mr. MacDonald was having his estate sale. Mr. MacDonald's wife Martha was only thirty-three years old when she died of a broken neck five months earlier by falling all the way down her back stair case. Mrs. MacDonald used to wear pretty dresses and expensive shoes whenever she came to our bake sales at George Washington Elementary School, so I thought there might be some nicer things to see at this particular sale.

By the time Bun and I got to the MacDonald's yard it seemed as though most of the better items had been sold. I remember seeing a worn-out summer dress with a pattern of yellow roses that Mrs. MacDonald sometimes wore. The dress was hanging over the branch of an apricot tree in front of the house. Underneath the dress there was an empty wooden crate and a brass music stand. On top of the crate I found a perfume atomizer and bottle which still had most of the perfume inside it, and nearby the crate on the grass there were numerous mystery books, harlequin romances, and an old rusted-out Raleigh bicycle. What immediately caught my eye and Bun's curiosity, however, was a pink patent leather purse sitting on top of a large cardboard box filled with wool stockings. Despite the black scuff marks on both sides of the purse I thought it was the most beautiful handbag that I had ever laid my eyes on. It looked just like the Grace Kelly handbags advertised in drugstore magazines. Bun started sniffing the purse like an old hound dog, so I left her with the bag and went over to ask Mr. MacDonald the price.

I knew what my mother would say if I brought this purse home. She would lament the fact that money did not grow on trees. She would remind me that I never wore handbags. She would tell me that I had wasted my money on an old, used, scuffed piece of junk. The word "junk" was a common word in my mother's lexicon. Despite her impending disapproval, when Mr. Macdonald told me the price for the purse was two dollars, I immediately handed him four quarters and ten dimes, my entire day's earnings from lemonade sales. I walked over and retrieved Bun and the handbag from the cardboard box. We then walked briskly back down the road to my empty lemonade stand where I had left a pitcher half filled with lemonade and melted ice.

I remember sitting down and staring at my prize in all of its pink shiny glory. I spat on the scuff marks and tried rubbing them out with my shirt sleeves. I next laid the purse on its side on top of the card table and watched Bun jump off my lap and crawl inside the purse's opening. I listened as she began scratching wildly at the inside pocket lining. At first I thought that there must have been some old cracker crumbs in the pocket of the purse which she was trying to get at. Soon, however, I noticed her tugging back and forth at an object which she had dislodged from the pocket, a folded piece of paper that she was finally able to pull out of the tightly stitched inner lining. When she finished liberating this folded paper from the inside pocket she let me remove it from her teeth. Although there were a few teeth marks on the paper, there were no tears. The paper had been deliberately flattened and folded numerous times before being placed inside the lining, thus making it difficult for both human and rabbit teeth to tear apart.

When I got the paper from Bun I was able to see that it had been carefully folded in quarters. The paper looked like it was removed from an old blue-lined school notebook. After I unfolded it I saw on the inside of the notepaper a single paragraph in small handwriting. Under the paragraph there was a date and the signature of Martha MacDonald, which had been made with a flourish of turquoise ink. The first line read as follows:

"If you have found this purse and this letter then I am probably already dead."

After I read that first line I began to feel a cold sweat. My heart started racing the way it does after Bun and I chase each other around the school yard. I felt nervous. I felt a little like I did the one time I helped a friend cheat on a math test by letting her copy my answers while the teacher's back was turned. Although I was elated at the prospect of a secret note, I also felt unsettled. I can't explain why I felt such panic, but when I read that first line I instinctively knew that what I was reading could cause someone a large chunk of trouble. I needed to shield its contents from everyone around me until I could figure out what to do.

The rest of the paragraph spoke of unbearable things, of occurrences that sounded too awful to be believed. Martha MacDonald wrote about how Mr. MacDonald would hurt her. She wrote about how he tried to strangle her two days before she wrote the note, when she was sitting at the kitchen table thinking about packing her bags and leaving. He grabbed her tightly around her neck, so tightly that she almost blacked out. The last line of the letter said simply: "I know he is going to kill me."

I looked carefully over the back and front of the paper to see if there were any other notations, but I didn't see any. Then I read over the paragraph three or four more times before stuffing it away into the back pocket of my jeans. I held Bun closely as I looked around to see if anyone was walking nearby on the road, but at that moment we were completely alone. I thought about going back to Mr. MacDonald's house to take a closer look at the mystery books he was selling at his estate sale. I considered how Mrs. MacDonald's note could have been written by someone who not only read a lot of mystery books but who was also trying to write one herself. Yet the more I thought about the way she was found five months earlier at the bottom of the stairs with her neck broken and her body crumpled up like a piece of discarded trash, the more I began to doubt that any of the violence described in the letter was fiction.

I needed to discuss this note with someone who would listen. I needed to talk to someone who would not immediately dismiss the idea that Martha MacDonald may have been murdered by her husband. The only confidants I had besides Bun were my two best friends from fifth grade, Angela Cartwright and Robin Morris. Both girls were members of a secret club we formed known as the Grasshopper Club. Angela, Robin, and I used to jump rope barefoot on the grass in front of the Glen Ellen Public Library so often and for such long stretches of time that townsfolk used to call us grasshoppers. The name stuck and we referred to ourselves as the Grasshoppers. Bun was an honorary member of the club and was quite good at jumping rope, as long as we didn't swing it too fast. Whenever we met we traded secrets, spied on neighborhood boys, watched movies at the Sebastiani Movie Theater, and perfected the art of jump roping.

The following Saturday I called an emergency meeting of the Grasshoppers. We gathered at the picnic table near the baseball field across from the local high school where Bun liked to chase gophers. I showed Robin and Angela the note Bun found. All three of us read it several times in silence. We pondered its authenticity. I then pulled out a photocopy of the original newspaper article I obtained earlier that week from the library, which gave a detailed account of Martha's death. The article described how Mr. MacDonald and a neighbor found Martha in a heap at the bottom of the stairs. It reported that an ambulance arrived within minutes after the discovery of the body. The article went on to describe the various contributions Mr. and Mrs. MacDonald made to our town, and gave the date and time of her memorial service.

We considered whether or not the note could have been a cruel school prank, but none of us really believed this. I thought about a detective show that Bun and I once watched on T.V. that was full of information about handwriting comparisons. The fact that Martha was dead meant that no police officer or private eye could ever take a proper sample of her handwriting in order to compare it to the handwriting in the letter. We talked about it all until it was time for lunch. It was precisely at noon that we came to the inexorable conclusion that Mr. MacDonald either pushed his wife down the stairs during a struggle, or tripped her on purpose, causing her to fall and break her neck.

We walked over to Angela's house. We were all hungry by then and we knew that Angela's mother could always be counted on to whip up something tasty for lunch. Mrs. Cartwright made bacon lettuce and tomato sandwiches for each of us, put a plate of lettuce and carrots on the table for Bun, and then left us alone in the kitchen. Robin was the first to speak.

'We can't let him get away with this.'

'It's been five long months since her "accidental death". No one saw anything. If I show Judge Reardon the note Bun found, would he actually believe that Mr. Macdonald, the man he goes trout fishing with every Sunday after church, did this terrible, horrendous deed?'

'Maybe you're right, but I'm with Robin. We can't let him get away with it.'

We went back to the picnic table after lunch and devised a plan to expose Mr. MacDonald as a murderer. For the next six weeks we stopped jumping rope on the grass in front of the Glen Ellen Public Library. Instead, we took our jump ropes and practiced outside Mr. MacDonald's house. Bun ran up to Mr. MacDonald's back door and scratched at the wooden door frame. This caused Mr. MacDonald to look out the back door to see who made the scratching noises. When the door opened Bun ran back to us and we started our jump rope practice in double time rhythms, over and over again. We sang out our rhymes in taunts just loud enough for Mr. MacDonald to hear from the doorstep.

We know what you did
We know you don't care
We know you pushed Martha down the stair!
The stair the stair the stair the stair
We know you pushed Martha down the stair!

Towards the end of those six fateful weeks it seemed like one of us was always running into Mr. MacDonald on the street in town. Sometimes Bun and I would see him at the grocery store or outside the ice cream parlor. Other times he would walk past all the Grasshoppers as we headed out to the playground. Once when I was walking to the post office to mail a letter he actually turned around and walked in the opposite direction after he saw me approach with Bun. During all that time he never spoke to us. For the rest of that summer we never stopped playing our jump rope games on the dirt road in back of his house. We never gave up trying to expose Mr. MacDonald and the truth of the mysterious handwritten letter.

When school started up again we would wait impatiently every afternoon until the final school bell sounded, signaling the end to our school day and the beginning of our late afternoon activities. I would run home, pick up Bun, and meet the other girls after school at the back of the MacDonald house. We held competitions to see who could jump and sing verses for the longest without getting tangled in the jump rope. We made up several different versions of what we called the Martha Rhymes.

Not last night but the night before
While on our way to the candy store
We saw you kick her and grab her hair
We saw you push her down the stair!
The stair, the stair, the stair, the stair!

By the middle of October we began to lessen the frequency of our after school taunts. Halloween was approaching and this meant that there were costumes we needed to sew and apples we needed to pick for the homemade pie and cider competitions, which our mothers always entered every October at the apple fair held in the Town Hall. It was the Friday before the fair when we first heard the news about Mr. MacDonald.

That Friday morning was particularly chilly when I got dressed and ready for school. Bun was scratching at the back door, wanting to get out of the house. I scolded her and told her it wasn't time to go outside and jump rope yet, that it was too darn cold to go out. I finally agreed that she could explore around the yard while I ate breakfast outside on the glider. When we went into the yard I was surprised to see her dig under the fence and head straight for Mr. MacDonald's house. I worried that I would be late to school, but I was able to catch her before she reached the end of my street. I took her home and put her in her crate, ignoring her protestations.

That same afternoon I went back to our house after school to get Bun. She jumped into my arms and went with me to meet Angela and Robin at the schoolyard. A boy we called Slider happened to be there too that afternoon bouncing a ball off a back fence near the kick ball court. As he looked over at us he stopped bouncing just long enough to ask if anyone had heard the news about Mr. MacDonald.

'What news?' I said.

'Old Man MacDonald went and tied a rope through the slats that separate the wooden planks on his back porch. Then he went and made a noose out of the rope. Then he went and hung himself! He went and hung himself right there by the back staircase! Right there, where his wife fell and broke her neck.'

I glanced at the others and then looked down at my feet. We left the school yard without saying a word and walked silently over to the MacDonald house. I thought about how Bun must have sensed that something terrible was happening when she dug under the fence in order to make her way over to the MacDonald house that morning. When we reached the house, I saw large strips of yellow hazard tape placed across the front door and side bushes near the back of the house. The large pieces of hazard tape kept flopping in the wind and reminded me of yellow tinsel on a Christmas tree. Angela was the first to speak. She said that we shouldn't feel responsible or bad in the least about what happened.

'He just couldn't live with himself because of what he did to his wife and now he's going to go all the way to Hell to pay for his deed.'

'Yes. It's that simple. He made his own bed and now he is lying down dead in it.'

I wasn't sure I agreed with either of them. I wanted Mr. MacDonald to confess the way detectives get bad guys to confess in the movies. My goal was to get him to admit to everyone in town how he killed his wife. I never wanted Mr. MacDonald to kill himself. I had always assumed that the justice we were after would be far less extreme. Now I held the secret to two different deaths, not just one.

I thought a great deal about Mr. MacDonald during the next few weeks. I felt heaviness, a moral burden that only comes from knowing a secret that cannot be revealed after the mystery is solved. I also thought about real life detectives who solve crimes, and realized that they, too, often carry with them this silent burden of knowing. I stuffed Martha's note deep inside the pink hand bag and hid the bag on top of the closet by the crawl space of my bedroom. Only Bun was allowed near it.

People talked for days around town about how Mr. MacDonald must have loved his wife so much that he just couldn't live without her. Most thought he died of love and loneliness. We knew better. I had hoped he would have left a note explaining everything, a note like Martha MacDonald's note, but none was ever found. Winter came that year with blasts of icy wind like at a funhouse ride, along with cold mournful fits of rain. After winter, spring crept forward almost out of nowhere and brought with it the sweet scent of pink jasmine and fresh green leaves on every tree branch in every park. Spring brought a kind of release from the heavy burden of those two deaths so many months ago.

By the time summer rolled around I was back at work with Bun setting up our lemonade stand. As soon as the August estate sales started up we went immediately over to Mr. MacDonald's house. His estate sale had been arranged by his older brother and sister, since the MacDonalds had no children. I looked at the pile of military books and maps that were displayed on a card table in front of his house and thought about how different all his books were from the romances and mysteries I saw there a year ago. I fingered a fine calf skin wallet lying next to some of his old shirts and boots. I wondered if some essence of a person remains in their belongings long after they die.

I remember feeling very sure at that moment in time that Mr. MacDonald was not going off on a long journey to Hell. I really didn't have any idea where he was off to, now that he was dead, but I knew where Bun and I were going. We were ready to go on and discover other hidden secrets and unsolved crimes. For us there was no turning back. The process of solving a mystery could carry with it an emotional burden, but we were prepared for that. We would continue to discover the secrets of other people's lives through old and worn objects. I said a quiet little prayer for Mr. MacDonald before we moved on to the next sale.

Time, Difference, Japan
Jason Jackson

YOU'RE THERE, ON the screen, which means you can be here, too.

You're saying that you went for a meal last night with someone called Kay and some of the other English teachers. You still can't stomach the food, and it's been almost two weeks now.

You're drinking from a can, and I ask what it is.

Don't worry, Dad, you say, *it's too early for booze. It's like grapefruit, but fizzy.* You try to say the name, and you laugh.

(…)

Dad, you say. *What's wrong?*

It's the screen, I say. *It still feels strange, somehow.*

You smile. *Hey, I've been thinking of writing you a letter.*

That would be lovely.

But this is cool, right? I mean, you're right here. I'm right there.

I say, *a letter would be good, though.*

You know what, you say, *I don't even know about stamps. They must have them here, right?*

Don't worry. This is good. It's incredible, really. Your mother would never have believed…

AND YOU START to tell me about the trip you're planning this weekend. You say the name of the place. It makes no sense to me. I watch you, on the screen, and you're smiling with the same lips, the same mouth, the same teeth. Those hands you have, those fingers that are pointing, and rubbing your chin, and running through your hair, I cut those fingernails, right here in this room, and because I was trying to watch the news—something about a bombing, somewhere, I recall—I cut too close and caught the skin of your middle finger, and you cried, dripped blood to the carpet, and your mother came in from the bedroom, asking what was the row, what was the bloody row about…

You're still talking about the trip. Someone has hired a car.
I say, quietly, *which side of the road do they drive on?*
What?
Left or right?
Left. They're like us, Dad.
They're not like us really, though, are they?
Dad, you say. *Are you okay?*
Tell me how much this thing costs again?
I've told you, Dad. It's free.
Doesn't seem right somehow, I say.
Anyway, you say, *what about you? What's happening your end?*
Oh, you know. Bowling. The club. It's been raining, so…
That's good, Dad. Listen…
Does it rain there?
Jesus, Dad, of course it bloody rains.
(…)
I'm sorry, Dad.
(…)
Dad, for Christ's sake.
It's fine. It's fine. I'm tired, Son. That's all. It's late here.
You smile again. *Time difference,* you say. *One of those things we've just got to get used to, eh?*
It's fine.
Okay, Dad. I'm gonna go now.

How do I stop this thing, then?
You laugh. *I showed you, remember?*
I'll work it out.
Okay. Bye, Dad.
(…)
(…)
And for a moment on the screen, there's a shadow of you.
A shadow of me.
And then the distance, again.

We Don't Understand The Machines We Have Created
Olivia Fitzsimons

SUBJECTS SET INSECT traps with yoghurt pots. Wandering like tiny Darwins across the dirty river, full of sludge and debris. Subjects hold their sticks with fabric high. Subjects are afraid. Subjects squint in bright sunshine and try to contain their giddy hearts filling with oxygen. We watch them with curiosity from the bank above. I think this cohort will do well. They are a favourite of mine. I, I, I, I rub my head, but it doesn't kill the itch. I straighten up and data appears on my visor.

Apples
Lemons
Mozzarella
Sky
Copper wire

I make lists in my network to pass the time. I make lists of things I think people want.

ON TUESDAY SUBJECTS find black blue beetles and spiders, trap the insects in the white pots and eat blackberries off the hedges. I long to touch them but I can't. We take notes and observe.

Sometimes subjects smile at me, like an inquest, are they doing well? I don't know if that is what they are thinking, so I pretend. I am bad at this part of the work. I am very bad. I am useless.

ON WEDNESDAY WE trap them as they try to leave. Subjects cry from the prison of the white pots. I cannot tell which is sadder, the beetles or the children and I worry again that I am not right for this task. Not suited. There is something missing from my program.

> Eliminate Population Waste
> Behaviour solution experiment
> Bamboo Nets
> Hair the colour of sea grass
> Nitrates

ON THURSDAY THEY are angry and crawl and struggle to escape. There is no point. Some fight until they are worn out. Participants talk to each other over the chaos. We observe them closely. Two tell stories of everything bright. Soon others listen. They calm everyone with their tall tales. Their words comfort against the wind. I check their identification numbers. I note variable behaviour. They are brothers. The data is tainted. I should tell someone.

ON FRIDAY THE group grows weaker but subjects sing songs that I do not know. I think they are songs. I have never heard songs *sung* before. Their voices are pure and beautiful and when they meld in unison I want to run to them, free them and let them be.

> *My bonny lies over the ocean*
> *My bonny lies over the sea*

My bonny lies over the ocean
Oh bring back my bonny to me, to me, to me

ON SATURDAY SUBJECTS start to die. It takes until Sunday for most to expire. I had thought this group would be stronger. When we do clear up, the bodies slide easily from the pots. Poor pitiful creatures. Perhaps the next study will survive longer. The brothers are almost copies of each other. I stare at them and when I put them in canvas, I put them together. I do not know why. I should not have done it but I did not want them to be alone.

While My Wife Is Out Of Town
Jude Brewer

TWO LIGHT BULBS burned out in the basement, so I used the flashlight app on my smartphone while carrying my cat with the other hand to ward off any ghosts.

I'm brushing my teeth in the shower while shampooing my hair and lathering my chest hair and the places on my back I can't quite reach, because I can't just stand in front of the mirror brushing my teeth doing nothing.

The four-dollar cinema is playing a documentary on cats in Turkey tonight, and I'm enamoured with their relationships, the cats and the people and how they depend upon each other, the cats for the food and the people for the soft company, but I'm also reminding myself that in three weeks the credit card bills are due and so is rent, and the car payment is due in three days, and I'm eating two delicious pizza slices.

I'm pretty sure everyone has been having ads broadcast to them in their sleep since everyone is drinking La Croix these days, and this is by no means an endorsement, just an observation.

I'm not feeling well so I'll hide like a house cat where no one notices, somewhere they can't ever find me, somewhere I can't hear the cellphone buzzing.

The dishes in the sink are getting crusty so I'll let them soak in room temperature water for five days while my wife is out of town.

The fresh smelling laundry is still warm and piled up on her side of the bed, so I'll play the big spoon.

The piano won't play itself, and my hand stabs the keys to see if a song can write itself, and the silence twanging off her guitars is louder than the empty fridge humming.

The pizza delivery guy just wants his tip, not an invite to hang out and play catch up on all these years we never shared; that's cool, maybe next time, next pizza.

The classics on my shelf could use a nice crease in their bindings so I tuck myself into this cooling laundry pile and feel my eyelids lower over blurring prose I've longed to live within.

These sneakers are cursing under my barking arches, and the autumn air rings with leaf blowers, and a chirrup follows my jog before, in one grand leap, I'm now chasing it.

On stage, a sixty-two-year-old-woman sings, her body contorting along with a pre-recorded track designed by an underground 70s band none of us have ever heard, and her voice wavers as the open mic host paces with his eyes darting around the room, like he can't decide if she should get a second song like everyone else has so far.

The bar's macaroni and cheese takeout tastes fine in the dark, in my quiet home, my cellphone buzzing, the screen's light filling my eyes, her message saying, "How was your day?"

AUTHOR BIOGRAPHIES

Tamar Hodes
Tamar Hodes was born in Israel and lived in Greece and South Africa before settling in this country. For the past thirty-three years she has combined her day job as a school teacher with her life as a writer. Her novel *Raffy's Shapes* was published in 2006 by Accent Press. Her short stories have been broadcast on Radio 4 and included in anthologies such as Salt's *Best British Short Stories 2015*. Her novel *The Water and the Wine* was published in 2018 by Hookline Books.

Karen Featherstone
Originally from Brighton, Karen Featherstone is a screenwriter and playwright, as well as a prose writer. A former health reporter, she has written storylines for Coronation Street and Emmerdale and her work has been featured at the National Theatre Studio and broadcast by Channel 4. She's a Write to Play playwright for Graeae Theatre Company, and is working on her first novel. She is a Channel 4/Lloyds bank screenwriting winner and Northern Writers' Award winner and a BBC ABBA finalist.

Sandra Arnold
Sandra Arnold is an award-winning writer who lives in New Zealand. Her flash fiction and short stories appear in *Flash: The International Short-Short Story Magazine 10.1* and *New Flash Fiction Review* and in the anthologies, *Sleep is a Beautiful Colour* (National Flash Fiction Day, UK, 2017), *Fresh Ink* (Cloud Ink Press, NZ, 2017) and *Bonsai: The Big Book of Small Stories*

(Canterbury University Press, NZ, 2018). Her flash fiction collection, *Soul Etchings*, will be published in June 2019 by Retreat West Books.

Dianne Bown-Wilson
Dianne Bown-Wilson was born in England, grew up in New Zealand and now lives in Dartmoor National Park. She has always written short stories (the first of note being 'Lost in the Dessert', at school). Her spelling has now improved and In the past few years several of her short stories have won or been listed in competitions including the Fish Short Story Prize, Writers Forum, Momaya, the Fresher Prize, the Yeovil Prize and the Exeter short story Prize. A collection of thirty-two of her successful stories, Instructions for Living and Other Stories was published in 2016.

Melvyn Elridge
Mel Eldridge is retired and lives on the south coast with his wife. With time and freedom, he writes flash fiction, short stories, crime thrillers and books for children. Shortlisted on several occasions in various genres he hopes his page turning-stories will find a publisher. A member of a local gym, perspiration leads to inspiration for his plots and characters.

Alison Wassell
Alison Wassell is a short story writer published in various anthologies, most recently the National Flash Fiction Day anthology *Sleep Is A Beautiful Colour*. Formerly a primary school teacher, she is now a part time seller of bottled gas for minimum wage.

Ian Tucker
Ian Tucker writes light and humorous stories for entertainment.

When he finds time he also tries to write whodunnit crime. One of his stories appear in the *What Was Left* anthology of winners from the 2016 Retreat West short story competition and others appear on his website tilebury.com. He lives in Bristol with his wife and a cat which has adopted her and the fridge.

Bettina Daniel
Bettina Daniel is working on a short story collection inspired by her walk along the Camino de Santiago de Compostela, a network of pilgrimage paths that end in Santiago in northern Spain, walked by over 250,000 people annually, from all over the world, for religious and other reasons. Each story is loosely related to one of the Ten Commandments.

Sarah Baxter
Sarah Baxter was born in Colchester where she still lives having returned after lengthy escapes to Australia and Scotland. In 2016, Sarah was second in Fish Publishing's flash fiction competition, and runner-up in Writers & Artists short story competition. In 2013, she was placed third for flash in 3 competitions: the Bridport Prize, Inktears and Flash500. Sarah has been long-listed for Bath and Brighton flash competitions. She has also been published twice by Words & Women for her short stories. In 2014, Sarah's work-in-progress novel won A.M Heath's 'Criminal Lines' competition. Sarah has a B.Sc. in Chemistry from Warwick University, which she says is invaluable when playing along with Pointless. You can follow Sarah on @UntoldFlash.

Laurence Jones
Laurence Jones was born and raised in London. His writing career began whilst studying American History, Literature and Creative Writing at Northern Arizona University in the United States. His short stories have been published in COLLAGES

(CCWC, 2013), an anthology of new writing, and NEW ZENITH MAGAZINE (November 2016), and STORGY (June 2018). He also won the Conville & Walsh Discovery Day event in 2013, was a finalist in The Literary Consultancy's Pen Factor 2015 competition and was longlisted for the LitRejections Short Story Prize in 2016. His story *Boys Outside* was longlisted in the 2018 Commonwealth Short Story Prize.

Shirley Golden
Shirley Golden's work has been published in various places in print and online. Two of her flash fictions were recently short listed in *The Casket of Fictional Delights* annual competition and are available as audio podcasts. She has self-published a collection of short fiction, which includes some of her prize-winning stories, titled *Exposing the False Moon*.

Joanna Campbell
Joanna Campbell is a full-time writer from the Cotswolds. Her short story collection was published in 2016 and was short-listed for the Rubery Book Award and long-listed for The Edge Hill Prize. Among various competition placings over the last ten years since she began writing, she was the winner of the 2015 London Short Story Prize, her flash fiction piece came second in the 2017 Bridport Prize and she won the 2018 Magic Oxygen Literary Prize.

Lucie McKnight Hardy
Lucie McKnight Hardy has a MA in Creative Writing from Manchester Metropolitan University. Her debut novel, *The Creed*, written as her dissertation for the MA, was longlisted for the Mslexia Novel Competition 2017, and the Caledonia Award 2018. It will be published in 2019 by Dead Ink Books.

Rachael Dunlop

Rachael Dunlop is an award-winning writer of short stories and flash fiction. Her stories have appeared in various places online, including Flash Flood Journal, Every Day Fiction, Words with Jam and Synaesthesia Magazine, and in several print anthologies, including most recently the National Flash Fiction Day anthology, Sleep is a Beautiful Colour (2017) and Stories for Homes 2 (2017). Her first (unpublished) novel was longlisted for the Bath Novel Prize 2017 and she continues to write fiction of all shapes and sizes, as the Muse strikes her.

Keren Heenan

Keren Heenan is an Australian writer and Arts teacher. She has won a number of Australian short story awards, and been published in Australian journals and anthologies, including: Overland, Island, Forty South Anthology, Award Winning Australian Writing, and in the Aesthetica Creative Writing Annual 2014, and Fish Anthology 2015 (Ire.)

Find her at: kerenheenan.wordpress.com or on Twitter @keren_heenan.

Susan Breall

Susan Breall is a judge working on cases of abuse, abandonment and neglect of children in the Superior Court of San Francisco. She is also a faculty member at the Book Passage Mystery Writer's Conference in Corta Madera California.

Jason Jackson

Jason Jackson writes short fiction and poetry. He also takes photographs. He hopes to find time in a busy life to get better at all three. Find links to Jason's published work at jjfiction.wordpress.com Jason tweets @jj_fiction.

Olivia Fitzsimons

Olivia Fitzsimons is a northerner living in Greystones, County Wicklow. She was shortlisted for the Sunday Business Post/Penguin Short Story Prize 2017. She has two feral children who she takes to the woods whenever she can.

Jude Brewer

Jude's writing has appeared in The Clackamas Literary Review, Scintilla Press, and Cultured Vultures. His nonfiction short, *2012, 2016, 2017* was a finalist in the 2017 Montana Book Festival. He also hosts a literary "radio theatre" podcast, Storytellers Telling Stories.

ACKNOWLEDGEMENTS

Thanks to all of the writers who send in their stories for the annual short story and flash fiction prizes and make these anthologies possible. We enjoy reading them all. Thanks to Louise Walters for reading the entries to help choose the long and shortlists, and to our judges Alison Moore and Tania Hershman for making the final decisions.

A special thanks goes to two of the contributors for travelling great distances to join us at the launch party – Olivia Fitzsimons who came from Ireland with support from Culture Ireland; and Bettina Daniel who flew over from the US, although I have a feeling the party was not the only reason! And also to our readers on the night: Joanna Campbell, Lucie McKnight Hardy, Tamar Hodes and Olivia Fitzsimons.

A big thank you to Jennie Rawlings at Serifim Design for updating the cover from the 2017 anthology, *What Was Left*. All of the winners' anthologies will have similar covers to form a series showcasing the wonderful work being created by writers from around the world today. But they are nowhere near as wonderful as the covers you design yourself, Jen!

Thanks to Phil Sobell for proofreading and his tireless work promoting our books online and beyond.

Amanda Saint

If you've enjoyed these stories, you can read more from some of the writers featured here, plus many other talented authors, in other Retreat West Books.

WHAT WAS LEFT, VARIOUS
20 winning and shortlisted stories from the 2016 Retreat West Short Story and Flash Fiction Prizes. A past that comes back to haunt a woman when she feels she has no future. A man with no mind of his own living a life of clichés. A teenage girl band that maybe never was. A dying millionaire's bizarre tasks for the family hoping to get his money. A granddaughter losing the grandfather she loves. A list of things about Abraham Lincoln that reveal both sadness and ambition for a modern day schoolgirl.

AS IF I WERE A RIVER, AMANDA SAINT
Kate's life is falling apart. Her husband has vanished without a trace – just like her mother did. Laura's about to do something that will change her family's lives forever – but she can't stop herself. Una's been keeping secrets – but for how much longer?

NOTHING IS AS IT WAS, VARIOUS
A charity anthology of climate-fiction stories raising funds for the Earth Day Network. A schoolboy inspired by a conservation hero to do his bit; a mother trying to save her family and her farm from drought; a world that doesn't get dark anymore; and a city that lives in a tower slowly being taken over by the sea.

SEPARATED FROM THE SEA, AMANDA HUGGINS
Separated From the Sea is the debut short story collection from award-winning author, Amanda Huggins. Crossing oceans from Japan to New York and from England to Havana, these stories are filled with a sense of yearning, of loss, of not quite belonging, of not being sure that things are what you thought they were. They are stories imbued with pathos and irony, humour and hope.

http://retreatwestbooks.com

Ingram Content Group UK Ltd.
Milton Keynes UK
UKHW022144030423
419589UK00015B/1058